SIREN SONG II

GEORGE DISMUKES

SIREN SONG II
Copyright © 2022 George Dismukes

ISBN: 979-8-88653-004-9

Melange Books, LLC
White Bear Lake, MN 55110
www.melange-books.com

Published in the United States of America.

Cover Design by Ashley Redbird Designs

This book is most reverently dedicated to my father, Sam Dismukes who named his boats "SIREN" and "SIREN II." Sam Dismukes, gone, but not forgotten.

PROLOGUE

by
Cheryl Peyton

Sixty miles off the coast of Belize lies the Great Blue Hole, the largest marine sinkhole on earth, at 1,000 feet across and over 400 feet deep. As seen from above, it is a circle of sapphire blue, edged by a necklace of coral, surrounded by a turquoise sea.

This deep funnel was formed at the end of the last ice age when an above-ground cave became flooded by rising sea waters. The limestone ceiling gradually weakened and collapsed, allowing light to reach into the interior of grottos that encircle the walls starting at 120 feet down to their floors at 150 feet. Stalactites and stalagmites are proof that the cave was once above water.

The site is a popular destination for divers with the

means to arrange for an excursion to this remote location, although only experienced divers are permitted to explore the underwater grottos that distinguish this prehistoric site.

———

Two years before the events recorded in this story, a group of residents from southeast Texas had signed on for a safari dive to the Hole, including: dive master and instructor, Ken Malloy, dive instructor and photographer, Scott Carrington, Scott's live-in girlfriend and business partner, Angie Holland, twelve-year-old James Harmon and his father Al Harmon, twenty-two-year-old deckhand, D J, and Gordon Hughes, the captain and owner of the *Siren Song*, a luxurious 80-foot yacht outfitted with all the finest SCUBA equipment and gear.

All of them had heard fantastic yarns passed down from old seamen about mermaids and sirens who live undersea, the latter depicted in Greek mythology as beautiful half bird-half women who lured sailors with their enchanted singing. Three of the group had been haunted by such images, while the others were receptive to the possibility of their existence.

Scott had a recurring nightmare of encountering a female beast in the Hole. On this dive, he planned to determine if she was real or imaginary; and to destroy her if she materialized.

Angie was just as anxious for him to solve the mystery so they could both have a peaceful sleep.

James Harmon had become obsessed with his family's legendary tale that his great-great-grandfather had been seduced and murdered by a siren after he ran his ship aground on an atoll during a storm. James believed the crash site was near Lighthouse Reef, the narrow barrier that encircled the Great Blue Hole, and that it was his destiny to seek revenge by finding and killing the siren. James's father, Al Harmon, a wealthy owner of a tanker company, had doubts about the veracity of the story, and hoped that James's dive in the Hole would be uneventful to free his son's mind to concentrate on his studies again.

Captain Gordon Hughes named his boat *Siren Song* after his father's two boats named *Siren and Siren II*. Gordon recalled when he was a boy he saw a live mermaid, or mer-human he thought was calling to him.

Head dive master and instructor, Ken Malloy, did not opine on whether he believed they would encounter a siren on this trip; he was more concerned with keeping everyone safe from the natural hazards in the Hole and the inherent risks of deep dives.

The last member of the party was twenty-two-year-old deckhand, D J, who seemed oblivious to tales of mermaids and sirens.

———

On a day in June, the passengers and crew of the *Siren Song* set sail for their destination in the Caribbean from the harbor at San Leon, Texas, on Dickinson Bay, where the yacht was berthed.

The night before, they had gathered at a *bon voyage* party that celebrated James receiving his Junior-Diver Certification from his instructors, Scott and Ken. The party had been shocked when a beautiful, exotic young woman

3

suddenly appeared at their table, introducing herself as Maris, and informing Captain Hughes that she would join them on the *Siren Song* the following morning.

Her abrupt departure left the group reeling with questions and apprehensions. Who is she? Where did she come from? Was she able to pay her way? A cloud of confusion then descended over them, rendering them unable to agree on her hair color, her age, or what she was wearing.

———

Suspicions and doubts about Maris continue as the *Siren Song* is underway since her certification card and passport are seen to be seriously out of date and lacking a photo.

An unfriendly Maris keeps to herself, keeping her distance from the rest of the party, apparently unwilling for them to know anything about her. The first night at sea she is able to keep her true nature a secret when she is unobserved repeatedly filling a glass with seawater and gulping it down to lubricate her inner gills.

After four days at sea, they reach the port city of Placencia, Belize, where the group stays for two days at Robert's Grove, an attractive seaside resort. At lunch the first day, an old man named Jenkins shouts a warning to the group from his wheelchair about a "blood-sucking, evil siren" who he says inhabits the Great Blue Hole. He explains that she had attacked him there and would have killed him if not for his daughter diving down to grab him. He hadn't enough air left by that time to avoid the bends that had left him crippled. When his daughter was later killed by a shark, his mind became unbalanced.

The first afternoon in Placencia, D J stays behind to watch the *Siren Song* while the group is taken by bus for dinner at an inland ranch owned by the resort. Once there, Maris discovers that her seawater had spilled out of her container and insists on being brought back to the boat for "medicine" she had left behind.

Back on the boat, she goes out to the dive board to fill her glass several times with sea water she drinks, but this time she is observed by D J who is standing on the pier. To keep her identity secret, Maris attempts to seduce him by stripping, and then singing to make him follow her, naked, into the water. Her kiss turns deadly as she sucks the air out of him. Morphing into the true self as a sea monster, she devours his face and head with her sharp fangs.

Meanwhile, back at the ranch, James shares a book he's found with Angie, titled *Folklore of the Caribbean*. It tells of a Greek siren who mates with a sea monster and gives birth to a daughter they "name for the sea" and send off to the Caribbean to live in an undersea palatial "chamber." James believes the daughter is Maris, as the name means "of the sea," in Latin, and that her lair is the Great Blue Hole. He further reasons that she wants to kill the whole party to keep future divers away from her home, but that he and Angie are safe as she is a woman and he is sexually immature.

When the party returns to the yacht, D J's absence is assumed to be due to his irresponsibility, so he is replaced with Chester, a Robert's Grove employee. The *Siren Song* heads out to view the Great Blue Hole via the Lighthouse Reef, to stay overnight at Halfmoon Caye.

The next day, prior to entering the Hole, James removes air from Maris's tank to prove that she breathes water; but it is his father, Al, who becomes distressed after injuring his shoulder and needs to be helped to the surface. Unseen, Maris calls a school of hammerhead sharks on the other side of the Hole. Seeing the fish, Angie, who's outfitted with an underwater firearm called a bang stick, manages to shoot and kill one of the huge sharks the others start to feed on.

After the divers get Al back on board and make him comfortable, Captain Hughes decides it's time to end the trip and head back to Belize City in the morning.

Their plans are dashed the next day when the boat's power lines are found to be shorted out and the radio inoperable. Going for help, Captain Hughes takes off in an inflated Zodiac, headed to nearby Halfmoon Caye, to call the Belize Coast Guard.

As he is underway, he hears a woman singing. Recognizing it as being the voice he had heard from the mer-human years earlier, he fights against the magnetism of the song that is sapping his will. Confirming his fears, Maris suddenly appears in the bow of the Zodiac boat, taunting him. In response, he condemns her for her murderous ways, accusing her of killing D J. Maris admits to it, but excuses all her killings as being necessary to save her own life.

Stating the inevitable, Maris suggests Gordon make love to her in the water to experience a last moment of pleasure before she takes his life. He pretends to be resigned to her plan but picks up an oyster knife before he drops over the side of the boat to meet her in the water. During her smothering kiss, he returns her embrace to bring the knife around to plunge into her shoulder. As he gets back in the Zodiac, he curses at the wounded creature and escapes.

Bleeding and in pain, Maris is still alive, due to her will to survive and her resolve to kill everyone else on the *Siren*

Song. Summoning all of her strength, she awaits her next victim.

She doesn't have long to wait as Ken enters the water to look for her since she hasn't returned from her swim. Feeling a tap on his shoulder, he turns to catch a glimpse of Maris as she wraps her tentacles around him, severing his head.

Up on the boat, James and Angie find a picture of Maris's image as a monster in Scott's camera, just as they hear him jump overboard. Looking down, they see Maris pulling Scott into the Great Blue Hole. James jumps overboard after them, armed with the bang stick. Crashing into Scott and Maris, he jars the instructor loose and confronts Maris. Feeling the presence of his great-great-grandfather, James discharges his weapon into the monster's chest. As Maris morphs between monster and woman, James fires again, striking her center mass. Maris finally succumbs to his attack and sinks into the abyss.

The next day, the boat's batteries have recharged enough to power the radio system. Gordon has returned to the yacht and calls the Belize Coast Guard. As they arrive to offer assistance, an unseen crown of feathers rises from the Great Blue Hole to stare at the *Siren Song* that floats above...

———

In SIREN SONG and SIREN SONG II, George Dismukes has done a masterful job of bringing mythological persons from the misty past into the present and allowing them to interact very naturally with his characters in both stories. He makes their presence in the 'here and now' seem, somehow, quite 'needed'!

You can see this fantastic tale brought to life on the big

screen when the movie is released to theatres nationwide next summer. It will star veteran actor Barry Corbin as Captain Gordon Hughes. A new rising star, Jenni Bahena Meador, will star as the siren. Her photo can be seen on the cover of the book, *Siren Song*.

See you at the movies!

CHAPTER ONE

We Saved Up Two Years for This!

Two years later

The Caribbean morning was crystalline. The sun had been up an hour, and the temperature was somewhere around 85 degrees off the coast of Belize; not that anybody noticed. On the stern of the good boat, *Lilypop*, the five passengers were gearing up for a dive.

The *Lilypop* had been so named by Bob Tagget, her owner, as an inside joke, a play on words, because he had a daughter named Lily. The seventy-foot Sea Shark was a sleek and proud sailing yacht, outfitted to the max for luxury. At the moment, she was resting comfortably, floating above the Great Blue Hole. As usual, the motors were idling, as Bob wanted to keep all the electronic equipment going as it hummed on the control panel, as well as the air conditioning to keep people comfortable. No passengers needed to worry about sweating needlessly when they were aboard the Lilypop.

There was general excitement in the stern this morning

as Bob and his wife Beth, and their three friends who had received their certification with them, pulled on wetsuits and strapped on their BCs, or buoyancy compensators, in preparation for this deep dive. The dive master, Lew Creighton, was standing near them and speaking in a raised voice to get their full attention as he recited some last-minute instructions; but nobody was really listening to him.

Bill Brady was examining his under-water camera to make sure all the settings were correct and that he had thought to insert a fresh memory card. He had waited a long time to dive into the Great Blue Hole, and he wanted to make sure he got some good pictures.

Ernie Falwell was checking all his equipment and pulling at his wetsuit, while Tom Barker was treating his mask with a defogging agent.

"Remember," Lew Creighton was saying, "Sometimes on a deep dive such as this one, people may begin to feel apprehensive, or even hallucinate. If you start to feel like that, do not hesitate to give me a signal and I'll escort you back to the surface. And under *all* circumstances, you must make a decompression stop at ten feet, to outgas. Tanks with regulator octopuses will be suspended in the water at the ten feet level for that purpose. There will also be an 'S' card attached there so you can check your time needed. It's all been covered in your classroom training. So... is everybody ready to go?"

There is a collective, enthusiastic *Yes*! One of the male divers was heard to say, with a slight laugh, "I can't believe we're finally here. We saved up two years for this!"

"All right," Lew said. "Let's get wet!"

As Gus the deckhand stood by, the five divers and Creighton fell backwards off the gunwale, into the crystal-clear water. Even though they had fallen in directly over the Hole, Lew had instructed them to gather at a point beside it called "The Slope" so they could make a final check to make sure their breathing apparatus was working properly. This done, Lew signaled that it was time to go, and the divers headed down the slope to the precipice of the Hole. Going over the edge, they began their descent. As with many divers who preceded them, there was a moment of anxiety resulting from the clarity of the water. Since they could see perfectly down to the thermocline a hundred feet below, it gave the illusion of having no support. This open space without shadow momentarily made them feel that they might fall.

That moment passed quickly, and they did indeed continue to "fall," albeit in slow motion, toward the milky white thermocline. The general feeling was upbeat, happy, and adventurous.

Then they entered the thermocline, a ten-foot-thick white blanket that gave the appearance of being a giant lid, sealing off what lay beneath the surface world. And what was beneath the thermocline were the grottos, the cave-like openings within the walls of this giant hole. The grottos were the ultimate destination of any diver who visited here.

The caves were ominous looking, and like a monster's opened jaws, were filled with teeth, which were actually the mineral formations formed thousands, perhaps millions of years ago, when the area was still above water, before the ice ages raised the water level and converted this place into a sub-sea wonder.

But the small dive group only had moments to be awestruck by this geological wonder, for tragedy was upon them in the form of a furious being that had lived for nearly two thousand years. The creature emerged from where it had been hiding among the hanging stalactites and struck. It didn't take long. Within a couple of minutes, all members of the dive group were no more. They had been turned into ravaged remnants, the victims of primeval outrage.

Now, the creature ascended, swam upward toward the surface, for there were two more humans to be dealt with, there, on the boat that had brought them all to this place.

CHAPTER TWO

A Disturbing News Story

L ittle Riviera is a small subdivision in San Leon, Texas, consisting of no more than fifty or sixty houses. Except for one row of houses near the beach, all of them flank both sides of a canal which empties into Dickinson Bay, an adjunct of Galveston Bay. Without exception, the houses are elevated on pilings ranging from ten to twenty-five feet high. They are what is commonly referred to as "beach houses," and the sizes generally range from eighteen-hundred to twenty-five hundred square feet, not counting the outdoor decks which, in almost all cases, are expansive. That's because this is Texas. And all Texans spend at least as much time out of doors as they do inside. Little Riviera is where Angie Holland lives with her boyfriend, photographer, Scott Carrington.

Their eighteen hundred square foot house features a huge deck that hangs over the canal far enough to create a cover for their small fishing boat, which is suspended above the water via a boat lift.

Inside the house, the walls are painted white and hung

with many framed photographs—copies of award-winning photos taken by Scott. Some are large, poster sized prints of stunning scenes from both above and below the water. Several books of Scott's photography are displayed on the coffee table.

It is early morning in the Carrington/Holland household. Angie Holland is in the kitchen, standing at the stove, stirring country gravy. She pauses long enough to brush her dark hair back and grab her coffee cup, which reads, "Bitch on a Mission," and takes a swallow of the hot, strong brew.

In one corner of the kitchen counter sat a small TV turned on to the morning news. Male and female co-anchors switch back and forth to report each story. The TV is 'there' but not garnering much attention from Angie as she prepares breakfast. Biscuits are in the oven and almost ready. Biscuits and gravy are Scott's favorite meal, especially if there happens to be a little sausage mixed in with the country gravy.

She raises her voice loud enough to be heard in the other room. "Scott, better get your butt in here. Biscuits are ready to come out of the oven."

Scott can be heard moving around in another part of the house. "Coming! I'm just trying to comb what's left of my thinning hair before it's gone forever. I wanna look pretty for you!"

"You look pretty enough," Angie says with a half-smile.

She takes another sip of coffee, then glances at the TV, just as a familiar sight comes on the screen. It is an aerial photo of the Great Blue Hole of the Caribbean. The voice-over news reporter says, "This just in; there has been an apparent multiple tragedy at one of Belize, Central America's premier heritage locations, the Great Blue Hole, located some seventy miles off that country's coast in the middle of Lighthouse Reef."

The picture changes to a wide shot of a yacht. "This dive boat, on a scuba diving excursion to the Great Blue Hole of Belize, was found several hours ago, floating, empty. The boat's motors were idling, but everyone on board has gone missing. So far, there's no explanation of why." The program returns to the news desk.

Someone, off camera, hands a sheet of paper to the female reporter. She looks at the paper a moment, then says, "Here's an update. One body has just been recovered. A male, believed to be a passenger on the trip, was found floating among the coral heads surrounding the Blue Hole, but has not yet been identified. The remains, apparently, are horribly mutilated. An autopsy will have to be performed to confirm the identity of the body."

"Mutilated?" the male reporter says. "Sounds like a shark attack. We'll break in the moment we receive any further information. This is Carl Craven, KTOK News, 'as it happens'."

Angie grows pale and drops her coffee cup that bounces off the side of the frying pan and lands in the gravy. She staggers. "Oh my God! She's back!"

Scott walks into the kitchen just at that moment. Approaching Angie from behind, he slips his arms around her waist. Looking over her shoulder, he says, "Who's back? What, no bacon? Did you know your coffee cup is in the gravy?"

"You don't need bacon. She's back!"

"Who? You keep saying that. Who's back?"

Angie points at the television set. "That murdering bitch from hell, 'Maris.' That's who."

Scott digs Angie's coffee cup out of the gravy. "Be serious. James Harmon blasted two holes into her. We were there. We both saw it. We saw her bleeding and sinking 'blissfully' into the bottom of the Great Blue Hole...forever! No more flying monkeys."

Angie's attention continues to be riveted on the TV. Walking over to it, she turns up the volume, to very loud. "Apparently not 'forever.' She's back."

Scott sets the gravy-covered coffee cup on the counter beside the stove and turns his attention to the TV set. The reporter gets deeper into the story.

"An intense investigation has begun. At this moment, we do have one remote camera on location. As you can see, multiple boats are arriving, including the Belize Coast Guard and the U.S. Coast Guard. We have information that seven people were on board the dive yacht. All are missing. As we reported a minute ago, one person has been found dead: the body, horribly mutilated. We go now, live, on location, with KTOK's own reporter, Ken Graham."

"I'm here, on an armed Coast Guard vessel which is actually tethered to the craft that is under investigation. With me is Brock Williams, special investigator with the U.S. Coast Guard. What can you tell us so far, Brock?" The reporter pushes his microphone toward the interviewee.

"Not much. At this point, the investigation is just getting under way. However, one strange observation is that there seems to be no damage to the craft itself, such as damage to the bow if it had hit a coral head. There isn't a scratch on it anywhere."

"So, what do you think did that to the body of the recovered victim?"

"Shark. Had to be a shark. There are some nasty

hammerheads that hang around in this hole. It was them. I'm reasonably sure of it."

Angie angrily turns off the TV. "Sharks, my ass. Sharks didn't do that."

"They did it at the U.S.S. Indianapolis," Scott says.

"That's because the U.S.S. Indianapolis sank, Scott. The Japs put two torpedoes into her. The boat went down and over eight hundred sailors wound up in the water. That didn't happen here. Didn't you hear? The yacht was untouched! It's her, I tell you. It's her. The bitch is not dead. *Somehow*, she survived two holes blown into her and a knife in the back. Resilient creature from hell. We should have known that you can't kill a two-thousand-year-old monster with twentieth century methods. We've got to fight her on her own terms."

Scott turns to Angie. "What? Her own terms? What the hell are you talking about?"

"I'm not sure. But you can damn well believe I'm going to figure it out."

"So…wait. I'm confused. Please define *her own terms*."

Angie heads for the door leading from the kitchen out onto the deck and to the stairway leading downstairs to the carport. "Eat your breakfast. I've got something to do." She slams the door behind her. A few moments later, the car in the carport can be heard starting, then backing out of the driveway.

Scott looks at the gravy. "Where's the biscuits? Oh, wait. The oven." He opens the oven door, takes an oven mitt, and slides the pan out containing the slightly over-brown biscuits. Placing the pan on the counter, Scott smiles. "Breakfast. Yeah!

Five miles away at a little league ballpark, fourteen-year-old James Harmon, dressed in a baseball uniform, stands, leaning face forward against the hurricane fencing that separates observers from the players in the batter's box. His hands are spread wide, clinging to the hurricane fencing as he watches his little brother trying hard to hit a ball.

"Keep your eye on the ball, Stevie," James yells. "You'll never hit it if you're watching seagulls!"

A girl, appearing to be the same age as James, is standing next to him. "Don't yell at him so much, James," she says quietly. Her name is Athena, and she has been James's girlfriend for the past two years. They met shortly after he returned from Belize.

"Sometimes, I can't help it," he says with a shrug.

The pitcher turns one loose and Stevie swings wildly, missing the ball completely. "Shit!" James mutters. Suddenly, he hears a familiar voice behind him.

"Hello there, big boy. Got a hug for an old friend?"

James turns to see Angie Holland behind him. A smile lights up his face as he reaches to hug her. "Angie! Oh, my goodness, how great to see you. Come here. Let me squeeze you!"

Angie returns the hug. "Good to see you, too. How are you?"

"Well, I'm trying to teach this little fart... mean, Stevie, how to bat. I may as well be trying to teach a monkey to play the violin. How'd you find me here?"

"I stopped by your house. Your mom said you were here. You look good in those baseball togs. So, who's this beautiful young lady with you?"

"Oh, Angie, this is Athena. We've been seeing each other for a couple of years now."

Angie looks at the young girl and smiles. "Greek?" she asks.

"Yes, ma'am," Athena answers.

"Well, I'm glad to meet you." Angie extends her hand in greeting.

"Thanks. So, what's up?" James asks.

"What do you mean?"

"I mean, I recognize that wrinkled brow, and the deep look of concern in your eyes. They aren't there by accident. So, what's up?"

Angie pauses, then steps up beside James to slip her fingers through the wire of the hurricane fencing. "James, we didn't kill her. That is, you didn't kill her. She's still alive."

"Impossible. I put two .357 slugs right into her brisket. I saw the blood. I saw her death throes. I saw her sinking into the bottom of the Great Blue Hole."

"I know, I know. I saw it, too. So did Scott. But somehow…"

"What are you saying? Somehow what?"

Angie stares out at the baseball diamond as she speaks. "There's a story all over the national TV news this morning about a yacht—a dive boat—found floating *empty* at the Great Blue Hole. There had been six or seven people on board. They found one of them. Apparently, a male passenger. The body was too mutilated for identification."

James looks stunned. He turns and grabs the fencing close to Angie just as Stevie connects with a pitch and sends the ball flying. Stevie turns to James. "Is that better?"

"Yeah," James says, "A lot better." Still looking through the wire, he slowly shakes his head. "I don't know what to say. If you're right, then that's terrible. But it's somebody else's problem at this point, right?"

19

GEORGE DISMUKES

Angie turns to look him in the eye. "Not hardly. How can you say that? You and I know what's going on down there. We have an obligation to tell those people what we know. She's a murdering monster, James. A merciless, mass murderer, completely without a conscience. This isn't the end of it. It's just the beginning. She'll never be through. She'll wind up killing hundreds of people. You and I might be able to help stop that. And you say it's none of our business? How can you say that?"

"Hold on! Hold on—you're right. I just hadn't had time to think it through. You're right, okay? We don't have any choice, do we? We've got to get involved. But exactly 'who' are we going to tell? Anybody we approach is going to think we've gone bananas!"

Angie bit down on her lower lip in thought. "Yeah, you're absolutely right. Oh, shit! We've got a major problem. And from the looks of things, now she's really pissed off and out for revenge. That's going to make her a lot more dangerous than before."

"What I'm starting to feel here is that we're going to have to get 'more directly' involved," James says.

"Yes, and more than likely, so does he," Angie said, indicating twelve-year-old Stevie at bat.

"Ohhhh, shit!" James Harmon says aloud. Looking upward, he calls out, "Great-Great- Grandfather, where are you? We need you now, for sure!"

"What are you two talking about?" Athena asks.

"I'll explain it later," James says. "It's complicated."

CHAPTER THREE

We Need a Plan

James walked over to the nearby bleachers and sat, forearms on his knees, looking down. "Are you sure it's her? I mean, like, absolutely positive?"

Angie sat down on the bleachers next to him. "It's got to be. Every detail about that news story matched her M.O.—the empty boat floating on top of the Great Blue Hole, the ravaged body. That's the exact thing that Gordon Hughes said she confessed to him—that her plan was for us. You know what, except for some very fortunate circumstances, and a lot of suspicion on our part, that could have been us on that news story."

James nodded in agreement. "Don't remind me. So, what do we do now?"

"I don't know. I need time to think. I do know one thing. There's an old proverb that says *to repeat the same mistake and expect a different outcome is the purest form of insanity.*"

"So then, no bang stick to the brisket," James says.

"It didn't work last time…apparently. She's a tough old broad."

"Well, she's a tough old something. That's for sure. Two bullets to the chest and she walks away."

"Swims away. And don't forget about the knife in the back. Guess she hasn't lived two thousand years without learning a trick or two. What we need is more information about her. But where do you find information about creatures from mythology? They aren't even supposed to be real. It's very doubtful that we'll find any DNA studies on them."

James listens as Angie talks but has no comment.

Angie turned to look at him. "That book you were reading in the library at the ranch house in Belize that night —did it go into any kind of detail besides her heritage?"

"Dunno. There were more pages about her, I think. But you and I got to talking…"

"What was the name of that thing?"

"The book? Uh, *Folklore of The Caribbean*, I think."

"I wonder if I can find it online?"

"Hah! Good luck with that one."

"Yeah, yeah, yeah. Well, I've got to start somewhere." Angie stood and started walking toward her car, kicking a pebble on the path. "I'm going to go get on the computer," she yells over her shoulder. "I'll call you. Stay close to your phone."

"Right," James says. "Really looking forward to it." Then, to his brother, "Okay, Stevie, can you do that again? Knock the cover off that thing!"

———

At home, Angie went straight to her computer and pulled up the Amazon website. Typing in the name Folklore of the Caribbean, she found nothing listed. She then looked on Barnes & Noble. No luck. She tried other bookseller websites. Same results. She then rooted out a 'rare books' website; one that specialized in old, and little known, volumes. No listing.

Frustrated, she closed the browser and went to the refrigerator for an unsweetened tea. Leaning against the counter, she opened the bottle and drank a mouthful. Pulling out a kitchen chair, she sat down and called Scott on her cell phone.

"Where are you?"

"At the gym, doing my workout."

"Okay."

"Why? Do you need something?"

"No. Well, yes. I need a fucking miracle."

"Okay. I'll stop at the Dollar store on the way home and see if I can find one."

"Cute," Angie said, ending the call.

She took another sip of tea and looked outside through the patio doors, toward the deck. The day was sunny. Only an occasional white, puffy cloud floated across the sky. Such a beautiful day, Angie mused, for there to be trouble anywhere on the planet. Much less a multiple murder in what should be one of the top vacation spots in the world.

If that crazy 'thing' had her way, bodies would be stacked up like cordwood. There was no question in Angie's mind that she was one of the few people on earth who knew the truth or had a possibility of stopping it. So, realistically, she had no choice. She had to "get involved", right up to her arm pits.

Angie suddenly sensed something near her feet. She looked down to see Pulga, her chocolate brown chihuahua, standing there, looking up at her and wagging her tail.

Angie reached down and scratched her gently behind the ears. "What you doing, little girl? You're always here for Mommy, aren't you? Bless your sweet little heart." She picked up the dog and held her on her lap. Pulga licked her hand.

Angie used her free hand to get her cell phone and called James Harmon.

"Hello."

"Couldn't find it."

"Not even on Amazon?"

"Especially not on Amazon. That's where I started. The book is just so old. It was probably printed somewhere in Europe, perhaps close to a hundred years ago."

"Well, don't they have other books on the same subject?"

"Yeah, but I didn't take time to check out any of them. Maybe I should have. I'll go back in and see what I can find."

"I wish I had some answers for you. But I thought this whole thing was over. I *hoped* it was over! It's *supposed* to be over."

"Yeah, no kidding. James, do you think you have been contacted by your great-great in any way? Maybe some subtle…something?"

"Umm, nothing that I can think of. I wouldn't be of any use now, anyway."

"Wrong. You have experience with this 'thing'. You have a history. There's far more knowledge inside of that head of yours than you realize. You can bring that to the table and help us find this monster's Achille's Heel. She's got to have one somewhere."

James was silent for several moments. Then, "Yeah, okay. I think I get what you're saying. But I can act as a consultant only. I'm too old to, you know. If I tried to go head-to-head with her now, she'd fry my bacon. I bet she'd like a chance to do that too!"

"Of course. Okay, Let's start by you helping me with this research. You've got more energy than I do, for sure."

"Okay, so basically, we're looking for the chink in her armor?"

"Exactly. Couldn't have said it better myself."

"And two bullets to the chest, ain't it. Cross that one off the list."

"That might be funny if it wasn't so true."

"Okay, let me get on the computer and see what I can find. You're going to be digging on that end too, right?"

"Of course."

"Keep your phone close. I'm probably going to have questions."

———

Angie spent the rest of the day deep in research on the computer. As she did so, her frustration mounted. There just was no hard-core information about the one topic she needed. She paused in the afternoon long enough to watch the evening news. Sure enough, the story about the empty yacht was everywhere, on every network, and on most local channels. An empty yacht found floating atop the Great Blue Hole. One body found. One reporter from Houston was astute enough to make the observation:

"There's something missing here, Carol," said a reporter to a fellow one at the station. "If this guy was diving, and I'm referring to the one body they have recovered so far, where is his dive equipment? He wasn't wearing a wet suit, a scuba tank, fins, mask. Well, there's no way to know about the mask for sure, but it's reasonable to assume, because the fact is, he wasn't wearing anything at all. Not even a bathing suit!"

Carolyn Brooks: "You mean he was completely nude?"

Bill Schultz: "What was left of him was, yes! As reported, the body was horribly mutilated. Some investigators on the scene feel that sharks are responsible. But the fact that he was naked strikes me as odd. I realize I'm not supposed to speculate, or editorialize here, but it's hard not to wonder and be amazed at the same time. This is one of the most beautiful spots on earth. And for such a horrific tragedy to occur here... Of course, the big question of the moment is, where are the other passengers? Six are missing—vanished! No trace of them anywhere and there are at least two dozen boats on the scene, most with professional scuba divers, going into the water...it's just very strange, Carol."

Carolyn Brooks: "Thank you, Bill. We'll be standing by." She turned to look directly into the camera. "This is continuing coverage of what is now being dubbed, "Mystery at the Great Blue Hole"."

Angie turned off the TV and looked out the patio doors as evening descended on South-east Texas. She picked up her cell phone from the kitchen table, which for the moment was serving as her desk, and called James.

When he answered, he said, without greeting, "No. I haven't found anything that will help us. You?"

"Not so much as a whisper. You been watching the news?"

"Yeah, I turned it on. The TV is on now, but I have the volume muted. I hate to admit it, but I agree with you that it's got to be her. Everything points to it, even the chewed-up stiff."

"James, don't talk like that."

"Sorry. Been watching too many cop shows."

"Well, this is not a cop show. It's a real-life tragedy, and a quandary."

"What do you mean?"

Angie exhaled. "What I mean is, this is a multiple murder. You and I both know it, and we have a moral obligation to do something about it. But who do we tell? Who can we recruit to help us go up against this creature? Can you imagine strolling into the local cop-shop and trying to explain to them that a two-thousand-year-old siren is responsible for killing a boatload of people? They'd take both of us away in white coats."

James nodded. "I see what you mean."

"Therefore, the only alternative, as I see it, is to find enough information about this bitch that we can put her away for once and for all. That is our *only* option. I don't like it, but there it is. I need to know everything there is to know about her. We know hardly anything. For instance, did you ever see her eat, even once?"

"No."

"Me, either. What does the bitch eat? I mean, I imagine that seafood is a good bet. But what seafood? She considers most sea creatures to be her friends, even those sharks in the Great Blue Hole. When does she sleep? For that matter, does she sleep at all? I want to know everything up to and including when she takes a crap, and how she wipes her ass. But the problem is so far I haven't found a frapping thing!"

"Calm down, Angie. You're yelling. It's hurting my ears, and besides, you're wasting energy."

Just at that moment, Scott came through the door leading from the kitchen to the deck. "Did I hear you yelling, or was that the TV?"

Angie turned to Scott. "It was me. Listen, James, I'm sorry. I'll call you later." Angie hung up the phone, dropped it on the kitchen table, and grabbed Scott's hand.

"Come with me," she says.

"Where to?"

"The bedroom."

"Because…?"

"Because I'm fixing to screw your brains out!"

Scott follows obediently. "I like your thinking!"

———

That evening, Angie stood at the stove, preparing dinner for herself and Scott, when her cell phone rang. She picked it up from the kitchen table.

"Hello?"

"You watching the news?" James asked.

"No, what's up?"

"They found another stiff. I mean, body."

Angie abandoned the stove and moved to the television set on the opposite side of the room. Turning it on, she tapped her foot nervously, waiting for it to warm up, then punched the cell phone's speaker button. "Who? Man or woman? Where were they?"

James's voice came back, sounding somber. "A woman. They found her in the grottos."

The TV screen lightened up, showing a male reporter on location. Angie turned up the sound. "The second body was found one hundred and fifty-feet beneath the surface, Jill. There are apparently some cave-like openings in the walls of this hole, which they refer to as 'grottos.' My understanding is that there are mineral formations within those grottos, not unlike the ones you see in caverns, and that is where the search team found the remains. That's as much as I know right now. The investigators aren't being very forthcoming with information at this time."

The woman at the station asked, "How many are still missing, Brad?"

"They think there were seven people aboard the yacht. But only five of them were passengers. The other two were the boat captain and a deckhand. They're missing too, which seems to rule out the possibility that this was a diving accident."

"It was certainly no accident," Angie found herself saying out loud. "And those dumb-bunnies will *never* find out the truth...and more people will be killed. I think she's gone on a full-blown murdering rampage."

"You may be right," James said.

Angie stomped around in a circle with her fists clenched. "I need more information. I need more goddamned information. And we're dealing with creatures who presumably don't exist except in some ancient bastard's imagination. Where the fuck can we find information?"

James Harmon was silent. He had no suggestions to offer.

Angie pounded her fist on the table. "I'm going to Belize. You wanna come?"

"My passport is attached to my dad's passport since I'm a minor. I've gotta talk to him."

"That's fine. But you didn't answer my question. Do you *want* to come?"

"Yeah, sure. Nothing's going on here. Not even on television, except re-runs of horse operas. Let me talk to Dad, and I'll get back to you."

"Make it quick."

"Okay." James disconnected the call and rubbed his chin as he stared at the television set.

CHAPTER FOUR

Return to Belize

The next day, Angie and Scott, along with James and Al Harmon were seated on a jet, flying at 30,000 feet, headed for Belize. Scott had the window seat; Angie was in the middle; Al occupied the aisle seat, and James was across the aisle from him, working on his laptop computer, earbuds in place.

After the flight attendant served their drinks and moved past them, Al turned toward Angie, scowling. "I thought we were through with this shit. My son has been put through enough. So have I. Last time we were down there, I damn near bought the farm because *something* knocked hell out of me in those grottos. It took a whole year to heal. Now you're dragging us back into it."

Angie's eyes widened in shock, hearing his words. Crossing her arms, she regarded her accuser with narrowed eyes for several seconds before speaking. "What?" she finally spat out. "I'm dragging *you* back into it? Let me tell you something, Al Harmon. I didn't drag you into a damn thing. If anything, it's the other way around. It wasn't my great-great-grandfather who had a run-in with that thing a hundred years ago. It was yours, or James's. I never went to Belize to get into a life-and-death battle with some friggin' creature from mythology. I went there to relax, get in a little diving, a little adventure, and watch my boyfriend take some pictures. Instead, I wound up in a tooth-and-nail battle with some demented, two-thousand-year-old something or other that has the power to seduce men with a song, and morph at will into a beautiful woman. Does that sound pretty accurate so far?" Angie shook her head in disgust.

Subdued by the woman's wrath, Al looked down at his rum and coke, his shoulders slumped. Taking a long drink, he turned toward her. "All right, I admit I hadn't thought about it that way. I'm sorry. I was out of order."

Angie continued to unload. "Here's something else to think about; you didn't get dragged into this; we all did. You think I want to be here? Does this look like I'm having a good time?" She brought her hand down in front of her face for emphasis.

Al shook his head. "No."

"We're here because we all have a moral obligation to try and stop this lunatic creature before she takes out an entire village of people. Or, she may have done that already. Who knows how many people she's killed over the years? And the problem is, there's nobody we can go to for help. Who's going to believe us? 'Excuse me, sir, but would you help us put the lid on a two- thousand-year- old creature from Greek Mythology? She really is dangerous. She kills people, you know, after she lures them into the water with a fucking song!'"

Angie sighed and ran her fingers through her hair. "God! What are we doing here? The whole thing sounds meshuga.

We're not going to get hauled off to jail; we're gonna wind up in the loony bin. And you know what? If we do manage to accomplish our mission, we won't be heroes. Because we still won't be able to tell anybody about it! So, this has to be the most unselfish act of our lives. What we are doing is for mankind, and "mankind" will never know about it! I must be dreaming!"

Al turned to Angie. "Exactly what is our 'mission'?"

Angie stared straight ahead. "To run this fox to ground and kill her. Really *kill* her, once and for all."

Al nodded. "I was afraid you were going to say something like that." He emptied his glass.

———

An hour later, the foursome landed in Belize City, cleared customs, and walked through the terminal to the domestic flights side of the building. There they got boarding passes for four on Tropical Airways and boarded a small, two-engine plane bound for Placencia.

A half hour later, they touched down on the landing strip. A courtesy van was there to drive them the short distance to Robert's Grove Beach Resort, where they were cordially greeted by their old friend, Dr. Maurine Howard.

After giving everyone warm hugs, Dr. Howard escorted them to the reception area. "You're already checked in," she said, smiling. "We just need to make sure which luggage goes to which room. Would you like to freshen up, or go straight to the bar for a liquid refresher? On the house, of course."

Angie needed to make a rest stop. Everyone else followed Dr. Howard to the bar as she made small talk along the way. "Michael will be here later. He's on a short fishing excursion with some guests."

In the bar, everyone was served a special cocktail called 'The Siren's Potion,' that turned out to be as tasty as it was colorful. The version offered to James was similar, but sans alcohol.

"It's not fair," James teased. "I'm fourteen. This is Belize. What is the legal drinking age here?"

"Eighteen," Maurine answered, grinning.

"Oh," James said. "Well, it was worth a try." Everyone laughed.

Just then, Angie rejoined the group, took a seat next to Scott, and tried a sip of her drink. "Ummm! Cold and a little sweet. Just right! What's this called?"

"The Siren's Potion," Maurine said with a smile. Angie nodded approval. "It was either that, or Michael's Madness," Maurine continued with a small laugh. "So, what brings you to Robert's Grove? Another trip to the Great Blue Hole?"

A raspy voice was heard speaking close by. It was Ol' Jenkins, and he was rolling his wheelchair straight toward their table. "Ha!"

As he bumped his chair against their table, he looked around with his one eye. "Ya didn't manage to kill her, did ya? You back down here to see what went wrong, where you fucked up? Well, you fucked up because she can't be killed! Not by no normal means, anyhow. Now she's out there, on a rampage, killing again. This time it was a whole boatload of people. She's gone crazy. She won't stop now, or ever!"

Ol' Jenkins was waving his arms and drooling as he spoke.

Dr. Howard motioned to one of her waiters to come get the old codger and return him to his own table.

"I'm sorry about that. But he's right about one thing—a terrible tragedy has taken place at the Great Blue Hole. Something happened to seven people. There are all sorts of investigations going on. All sorts of wild theories. Access to the area is shut down. Nobody can go any closer to the Hole than Halfmoon Caye. We've got reporters from several media sources staying here." She indicated the nearby swimming pool where several people were sun-bathing or swimming.

Angie looked thoughtful as she took a sip of her drink. "You know about our last trip down here, right?"

Maurine nodded. "Yes, Michael filled me in once I got him drunk enough. He didn't want to talk about it for a long time."

Angie nodded knowingly. "Well, 'Tragedy at The Great Blue Hole' is the top news story on every station in the states. It's a wonder you aren't overrun with people snooping around. Anyway, it's the reason we're here. The only difference being, we aren't just curious tourists."

"So, why *are* you here?" Maurine asked with raised eyebrows.

Angie glanced over at James as she answered, "We…'I', want to go to the ranch. There's a book there that James came across on our previous trip. It's called *Folklore of The Caribbean*, and I'm looking for information that may be in it. I'm not sure, but maybe."

Maurine blinked. "You came all the way to Belize to read a book?"

"Not just '*any*' book," Angie said. "*That* book."

"Okay. I'm sure you have your reasons. I'll have Tontoni drive you out there in the morning. Will you want to stay overnight at the ranch?"

"No. I don't think so. I need to plow through that book to see if I find what I'm looking for. One way or another, I don't think we should be more than a couple of hours. Then we'll need to come back here."

"Very well. I'll instruct Tontoni to wait for you."

"Thank you," Angie said. "We appreciate your help very much."

Al Harmon cleared his throat. "Look, I can see I'm gonna wind up out there sitting on my rear end while you two are reading. I think I'll stay here and maybe drown a shrimp or two. I've seen some fish schooling over there in the harbor. They might have been snook."

"Me too," Scott said. "I'm going to wander around the village with my camera. I didn't get to do that the last time we were here. I already see some things that might translate well."

Angie's mouth twitched in annoyance. "Okay, fine. You and Scott stay here. James and I will do the research. You're right—you'd just be in the way and bored. Oh wait, let me reverse that. You'd be boring, and in the way."

Al pulled at his collar. "You hear that, Scott? Just like Rodney Dangerfield, we get no respect!"

Scott nodded in agreement.

From across the room, Ol' Jenkins yelled, "You better watch your ass! She knows who you are now, and she knows why you're here. She'll be gunnin' fer ya!"

Under her breath, Angie said, "Crazy old bastard just might be right."

"Goddamn right, I'm right," Ol' Jenkins yelled back.

Angie's mouth fell open. "You heard that?"

"Yeah, I heard it. It's my legs that don't work, not my ears. An' I ain't nearly as crazy as ya might think. I'm sane enough to know you're walking into a rattlesnake pit without boots on. Mark my words... she's laying fer ya this time."

"Let's get out of here," Angie said as she balled up her cocktail napkin and rose from her chair. "I've heard enough prognosticating from that old fart."

As the foursome left the bar, followed closely by Dr. Howard, Ol' Jenkins could be heard, cackling to himself.

CHAPTER FIVE

At the Ranch

Totoni pulled up in front of the ranch house the next morning and turned off the van's motor. Angie just sat there for a moment, staring out her window. The ranch house looked desolate and empty; maybe even a little spooky. Angie pushed down her misgivings and opened the van door. "Okay," she said. "Let's get this show on the road."

Tontoni raised his hand in response but stayed in the van. "I be here if you need anyting."

Angie used the key given to her by Dr. Howard to unlock the door. "Well, this is what we came to Belize for," she said to James. "Let's get this done."

James followed her as she made her way through the house to the library, turning on the lights with all the switches she could find along the way. Good! The electricity was working. Finding the thermostat, she turned on the air conditioner. The soft humming sound of the AC compressor was somehow reassuring.

Looking around the orderly, lit-up space, she smiled. "That's more like it. Okay, let's get to work."

James was already scanning the rows of books on the shelves. It didn't take very long before he located the one volume he was looking for.

"Bingo!" he called out after a minute or two. Angie's eyes widened with interest as he carried the book to the reading table located in the middle of the room. Putting it down, he opened it to the approximate place where he remembered reading two years earlier.

"It's gotta be here someplace," he muttered, flipping through the pages. "Okay, here it is."

Angie grabbed the book from him and began reading the page it was opened to, sinking into a chair as she did so. After a half hour, she pushed the book back to him across the table where he was reading. After thrumming her fingers on the table for a few seconds, she stood up and paced back and forth a few steps.

Walking over to James, she pointed to the book she had returned to him. "There isn't one word in there about the siren's weaknesses. Seems to me that when I read stories from mythology, there was always some weakness or other that allowed the hero, or good guy, whatever, to kill it. Even Medusa, for example. Thinking back to my college days I remember she was beheaded with the Sword of Hermes. But it wasn't that simple. Seems like he needed a magical shield of polished metal that was like a mirror that reflected Medusa's image back at her. She needed to see her own image before she could be killed.

"I think we're up against the same kind of problem here," she continued excitedly. "There has got to be some special something...maybe a formula that lowers the invisible wall that protects Maris."

"I hear what you're saying. So, what would that be?" James asked.

Angie dropped down in a chair next to him and sighed. "I don't know. That's what we've got to find out, and I don't have the slightest idea where to look. This might be the most important thing I've ever done in my life, and I'm as lost as a goose in a snowstorm."

———

Back in Placencia, while Angie and James were in the library in the ranch house rifling through books like *Folklore of the Caribbean*, Al was standing on a pier behind Robert's Grove Resort holding a fishing pole, casting into a swirl in the water some forty feet away that looked to him like fish schooling. He was wearing his favorite flop hat, Bermuda shorts, and a T-shirt that read "Reel Fisherman" across the front. He was already sweating from the Belize heat.

He was relaxed and thinking about nothing other than whether or not he would get a strike, as he artfully moved his lure across the surface of the water. It would be nice to have a fish on the grill that he had caught. That way, he would be sure how fresh it was. Fresh fish was one of his favorite things in the world.

Behind Al, underwater, something moved slowly, cautiously, silently, toward him. Whatever it is, it surfaces scant feet behind him and raises itself up onto the pier within an arm's length of the big man, noiselessly, without alerting Al.

Al was surprised and caught a little off guard when he heard a soft, female voice behind him ask, "Are they biting?"

Turning his head, he sees a petite brunette standing there. She is of slender build with long hair that hangs down to her waist and looks to be in her mid-twenties at the most.

"Not yet," Al replied. Cocking his head to one side, he asks, "Who are you?"

"I'm Mara," the girl said, smiling.

"Hello, Mara. Are you staying here at Robert's Grove?"

"No. I'm on a yacht, down the beach a way."

"Are you one of those reporters here to cover the thing going on at the Great Blue Hole?"

"No, but I am here because of what happened out there."

"Oh? In what capacity?"

Mara shaded her eyes with her hand to better see someone who was waving at her from a hundred yards away. Mara waved back, then turned to leave. "I'm sorry. I have to go now," she said. "I'll talk to you later."

"Okay," Al said, but he repeated his question after she turned and started walking away. "You never did say why you're here."

"To help," Mara said over her shoulder.

"What?" Al asked, now suddenly more interested. Mara stopped and looked back at him.

"To help," she repeated, then turned and continued walking away, leaving Al Harmon puzzled by her words.

———

At the ranch, Angie and James continued searching the bookshelves for anything else that might be of help, but they were coming up empty-handed and had become discouraged.

Standing and staring blankly at the wall of books, they heard an elderly female's voice behind them. "The answers you seek cannot be found in the pages of those old testaments."

Angie wheeled around, shocked to see the speaker—a shriveled old woman bent over from arthritis, dressed in long, black clothes like widow's weeds, who stood in the entryway to the library. The woman's eyes were faded with age, her hands wrinkled. She took a step into the room.

"You want to know how to kill her. But your answers are not there. You can look until doomsday. Save yourselves the trouble. Look no more. You're going to need your energy for other things."

"Who are you?" Angie demanded. "And how do you know what we're doing? For that matter, how did you get in here?"

The old woman hobbled forward and slumped into a chair on the other side of the reading table. Peering at them through rheumy eyes, she continued, "You're focused on the wrong things. I got in here through the front door. It was open. It doesn't matter how I know, what I know. It only matters that I know. And I'm here to help you accomplish your mission. But you must listen very closely to what I tell you and follow my instructions precisely. Otherwise, you will fail, and she will go on killing, starting with you."

––––––

Dinner that evening was a mixed bag of emotions. Al was pleased with himself because he had caught two rather large robalo (snook), which he had meticulously cleaned and turned over to the cook at Robert's Grove who promised to turn them into a feast. By now, Al was celebrating his triumph with Scott who was at the approximate same place emotionally, and equally inebriated.

Scott, too, had enjoyed a successful day. "You wouldn't believe all the things there are around here to photograph. Some of the colors of these old houses just scream *CARIBBEAN!*" he said, laughing. "I got some great shots! Just great!"

Angie and James were both quiet and looked preoccupied. Angie sucked on a straw that was in a tall 'Siren's Potion' glass in an attempt to make herself feel better. The results were limited. James seemed far away, munching on bread while he waited for the fish to be served.

Addressing Angie, Al asked, "How did things go at the ranch today?"

"Surprisingly well," she answered.

"Oh? Good. Does that mean you found the information you were looking for?"

"In a manner of speaking," she acknowledged, taking a piece of bread from the basket and smearing some butter on it before taking a big bite.

Scott studied her for a long moment, curious about her mood. "You aren't being very forthcoming. I thought we were in this thing together. What gives?"

Angie munched on her bread, swallowed, and took a gulp of Siren's Potion. "Somebody has to die."

Scott didn't skip a beat. "Well, of course. That's what we're here for, isn't it?"

"No. Somebody besides the siren has to die."

"What the hell does that mean?" Al asked.

Just then, Scott's ring tone sounded on his cell phone. Removing the instrument from his belt saddle, he answered, "Hello? ... Yes, it is ... Yes ... (long pause) No shit! Wow!

That sounds like an interesting project ... Yes, I would, but Angie Holland is my business agent. You will have to make those arrangements through her...sure. As luck would have it, she's right here. I'll give her the phone."

Scott handed the phone to Angie. "Who is it?" she whispered.

"The Science Analyst Magazine," he whispered back. They want to hire me for a special job."

Angie took the phone, then got up and walked away for several feet to continue the conversation. After speaking to the caller for several minutes, she returned to the table after hanging up the call. "You're going to Africa," she said to Scott.

Scott raised one fist in the air with a triumphant, "Yes!"

Al returned to Angie's last remark before Scott's phone call. "So, what did you mean by, 'Somebody besides the siren has to die'?"

"It's complicated," Angie said softly. "Very mother fu... it's complicated. I don't think it's a good idea to get into it here. I'll explain when there aren't so many ears around."

Right then, the fish feast arrived, and it was everything the chef had promised. He had buried the baked fish in a cluster of shrimps, flavoring the mix with slightly sweet spices set off by a lemony note. The whole mixture thing was surrounded by a circle of braised veggies, several inches high, including mushrooms, tomatoes and brussel sprouts.

All conversation was tabled for the moment while the hungry group dug in accompanied by the sounds of oohs and ahs.

———

Angie had drunk too much Siren's Potion with her dinner since the concoction went so well with food, but the alcohol caused her consternation to begin to bubble to the surface.

After dinner, she rose from the table to make her way to a table on the outside deck, which overlooked the harbor. Plopping down in a chair, she gazed out at the water as the sun went down. "Ooohh, my God, what a delicious meal," she said aloud. "I've gotta get that chef's recipe!"

Scott had joined her, quietly settling into the chair next to hers. "Something you want to talk about?" he asked after a minute of looking out to sea. "Like maybe, Africa? When am I going? How much are we getting paid? How long am I supposed to be there? You know, unimportant little things like that."

Angie continued staring at the water, the yachts, and the cayucos, which were beached a hundred yards away. "You leave in the morning. They want you to take pictures for a piece they're doing called, 'Where Hurricanes Are Born.' I'm not going with you. I've got to finish what I've started here. The job will last a minimum of two weeks. You're getting paid three K per day plus per-diem."

Scott looked crestfallen. "You're not going with me?"

Angie turned her head to look at him. "In case you haven't noticed, I've got a pot to stir right here in Belize."

"Yeah, but it'll be here when you get back."

"And how many more people will die in the meantime, while I'm watching you work, Scott? Just so I can be a tourist and your fan club along the west coast of Africa? Don't you think an attempt to save lives takes precedent over that?" she asked through clenched jaws.

"Yeah, you're right," Scott agreed. "It's just that I'll miss you, that's all."

"It's called co-dependence," Angie said accusingly. "Get over it. Sometimes, things are important enough that they override co-dependence."

Angie saw that her words had hurt Scott, and she softened. Reaching over, she put her hand on his arm. "Get that whipped puppy look off of your face. I love you, Scott, or I wouldn't be with you. But this is important, honey. If I'm right, it means that damn siren has gone off of her toolie. She's paranoid. She thinks the whole world is out to get her, so she's going to fight the invisible dragon the only way she knows. She's insane, but she's also cunning. She has to be stopped."

"Well, that's what worries me. You are going to take on this bitch from hell and I'm not going to be here to help?"

"You're going to be gone for two, maybe three weeks. Who knows if we'll even be any closer to solving this riddle in three weeks? Go shoot your magazine story. We need the moolah. Then, come back to me. Just imagine what it will be like when we're back together after a three-week separation."

Scott smiled as he thought about Angie's words.

———

The next morning, Angie, James, and Al waved goodbye to Scott as his small Tropical Airways dual-prop plane lifted off from the runway at the Placencia airport.

As the plane grew smaller in the sky, the trio turned around to get into the limo to go back to Robert's Grove. Once inside the vehicle, Angie moaned, "What the hell are we doing here?

"What do you mean?" Al asked, looking confused.

"I mean…what are we doing here in Belize? This is obviously someone else's problem. So, why did I think, of all the people in this world, that *I* could come here and fix it? What kind of ego is that?"

"I don't think it's ego driven," Al said. "Just maybe you care more about people than you want to admit to yourself. Just a hypothesis, understand!"

"Oh, horse shit, Al! Sure, I care about people, but it's no big secret. I don't go around wearing my heart on my sleeve. No. This is more like…something unfinished. Your son put a bang stick in that bitch's chest, with, I might add, the help of his great-great-grandfather and blew two holes in her. He did it. I saw him.

"Yep," Al responded, grinning.

"Yeah. And we all saw her sinking like a river rock into the Blue Hole. Blood was leaking out of her like oil out of an old Ford; and, yet…*surprise!* The bitch is back, and apparently now with a hard-on because she's taking people out by the six pack. We didn't finish the job, and now other people are paying for our failure with their lives."

"Wait! You blame yourself for that? Because that's not right. None of this crap is your fault. So quit beating yourself up," Al said. "That's more than a little counter-productive at this point, anyway. Our total focus needs to be on the solution, not bitching about the problem."

"I know you're right. You are. But I just can't get around feeling a little guilty about it. I feel an obligation to do something to stop her. Hence, this safari to Belize. And now, here we are, ensconced at Robert's Grove Resort, wondering who she's going to slaughter next!"

"Wow. Talk about putting a negative spin on it."

"It's no 'spin,' Al. It's the cold, hard truth. While we're

sitting around the bar at the resort, sipping Siren's Potions, relaxing, making chit chat, she's somewhere out there, zeroing in on her next victim, and she's never going to stop. Those are the facts, like it or not." Angie peered out the window of the limo as it steered back toward the resort. "Sorry. You're right. We need to be focused one hundred percent on the solution. I just get frustrated at the pace by which we are doing it.

"I've got to do 'something,' and I don't know what in the hell to do! When we were at the ranch house, this old crone showed up out of nowhere. She wasn't there, and then she was there, standing in the doorway to the library, all dressed in flowing black. It was surreal, like something out of a goddamned ghost story. Anyway, she starts telling us all of this stuff we need to do to kill the siren. I'm talking about 'really' killing her. She said there was some kind of a chant, I guess, that the person closest to her has to recite..."

"A chant? That's all? That's it? That don't sound so bad."

"Wait. I'm not through. Here's the good part! The person who does this chant must then allow themselves to be killed by the siren. *Killed!* Killed by the goddamn siren."

Al stared mutely at Angie with his mouth open, trying to absorb what she had just said. The movement of the limo on the uneven road and the passing scenery were suddenly inconsequential. "A sacrificial victim?"

"That's what the old babe said, yeah. So, any volunteers that you can think of right off the top of your head? Does this qualify as a conundrum?"

"Well now, wait a minute. I mean, just how credible is this old woman. You don't know her. She just 'shows up'? She could be as full of shit as a Christmas turkey."

"No...no. She knew things. For instance, how did she

know why we were in that ranch house? Not even that driver, uh, Tontoni, knew why we were there. All he knew was to drive the van because Dr. Howard told him to do it."

"So, 'that' gives her credibility?"

"You had to be there."

The limo pulled up in front of Robert's Grove and the trio bailed out to make their way to the deck in front of the bar. James followed in silence, listening to the dialogue between his dad and Angie. On the deck, he picked a table and plopped down in a chair to look out at the water, needing to squint at the rising sun. Al and Angie also took a seat, but not for long.

Al rose from his chair and walked to the railing of the deck. Standing with his hands on his hips, he looked back at Angie. "So, what's next?"

Angie shook her head as she looked out at the water. "I don't have the slightest idea in the world. I'm as lost as a goose in a snow-storm. I thought I was a problem solver. But this one's got me. All I know for sure is, there has to be an answer somewhere. I wonder if that old crone has a crystal ball?"

Al chuckled. "Do you know how to get in touch with her?"

"No," Angie said, shaking her head. "She walked around the corner, out of the library. I chased after her to ask her one last question, but when I reached the doorway and looked down the hallway, she was gone."

"Gone? Why do I have the feeling there's another word that you aren't using?"

Angie raised her voice slightly. "Disappeared. Okay, Al, you happy? Disappeared. The fucking old bitch just disappeared. I mean, I was right behind her by no more than *eight feet*. She walked around the corner, and 'poof' she was gone. The very last thing she said to me before she walked out of the room and disappeared was, 'There's one more thing...' That's why I chased her. I wanted to ask, what 'thing'?"

"Sooo, we're dealing with spirits here? Twilight Zone stuff?"

"Shit, I don't know. Maybe. Why not? It's no crazier than any of the rest of this." Angie shook her head. "We're dealing with a siren who isn't supposed to exist, except in myth. Why not a spirit, or a witch, or a curandera? I'm out of my league with all this. Maybe we should just go back to San Leon and let someone else worry about it. God knows, there's enough people out there at the Blue Hole."

Al looked down and grunted. "Yeah, that sounds good, in theory. But none of those people have any idea what the hell they're doing either. At least you know what the true situation is. And I'll tell you something, from what I know about you, it wouldn't matter what it was. Once you bite down on it, you aren't going to let go until you have the conundrum, as you put it, solved. I saw it on our previous trip down here. And this...well, this is a very big, 'what it was'."

Angie rose from the table and started walking toward the restaurant/bar. "Tomorrow, we're going out to the Great Blue Hole."

Al looked up at her with raised eyebrows. "What? We can't do that. They've got the whole area cordoned off. No access to anyone, remember?"

"Yeah, well, we've got some work to do, so get ready to pull a rabbit out of a hat."

Al's eyes rolled toward the sky for a moment. "Oh shit,

oh dear. Angie, you're going to get us in trouble right up to our asses!"

"No guts, no glory." Angie said over her shoulder as she continued on toward the bar. Then, stopping and turning to look back at him, she added, "First, we need to make one last stop at the watering hole in here, because I need to get just a little plowed before we do anything else."

Al stood and hurried after her, leaving James sitting at the table. "I'm all for that. After all, it's gotta be five o'clock somewhere in the world. Besides, if I'm gonna go to jail, I don't want to go sober."

When they walked into the restaurant, they heard Reggae music playing softly from a rather large and elaborate boom-box that sat at one end of the bar. The bartenders were laughing and having a relaxed conversation with a patron whom Angie hadn't seen before.

The stranger was a tall man with an olive complexion, built like an athlete, with a thick mop of hair, as black as midnight. He had a contagious smile and when he glanced over at Angie to nod and acknowledge her, she froze and felt things she knew she shouldn't be feeling.

Angie looked away, which took an effort, and tried to order her drink, but found that she was shaking, her voice trembling slightly. "I need a rum and coke, please. Easy coke."

"Coming up," the bartender said with a smile.

Angie climbed into one of the captain's chairs at the bar. Al took the one next to her. "What's going on?" he asked.

"I don't know," Angie lied. "I think fatigue is beginning to set in."

"This early in the morning," Al said.

"I didn't sleep good last night," Angie explained. "Scott was restless because he's leaving this morning."

"Hello," someone said on her left.

It was the handsome newcomer, extending his hand in friendship. "I didn't mean to ignore you. My name is Dimitri Mykos." He spoke with a delightful Greek accent.

Angie swiveled her captain's chair toward him and extended her hand. "Hello. I'm Angie Holland. And this is Al Harmon."

"Are you staying here at Robert's Grove?" Dimitri asked.

"Yes," Angie responded. Then she went silent. She was rarely at a loss for words, but this was one of those times.

Al looked past Angie at Dimitri. "So, what are doing in these parts? You down here on a dive trip?"

"Well, sort of. I am a diver—a cave diver. I've been hired to search for those missing people out at the Great Blue Hole."

"Yeah," Al said. "That's a sad situation. What do you think happened to them?"

Dimitri looked down and smiled. "Well, I have my own theory, just as you do. But the main thing now is to locate them if we can."

Angie broke loose from her trance. "What do you mean by "just as you do"?"

"Well, don't you?" Dimitri asked. "Doesn't everybody in this part of the world have one theory or another? That's only natural."

Angie hesitated. "Yeah…I guess you're right about that."

The bartender placed Angie's drink in front of her. She seized the glass and turned it up, drinking the whole thing, nonstop. Setting the empty glass on the bar, she said, "Well, nice meeting you." Sliding out of the chair, she added, "I'm gonna call it a night. It's been a long day and a frustrating one. So... I'm going to hit the sack. Maybe tomorrow will be better."

"Why are you going to bed, now?" Dimitri asked. Gesturing toward the outside. "It's morning. The sun has barely come up."

"Oh...yeah." Angie said, looking toward the water. But there was no bright day emerging. Dark clouds were rapidly moving in. It *is* morning," she said, seeming surprised. "Whaddaya know." She climbed back into her captain's chair.

As if to punctuate her words, a thunder-clap walked across the sky. That one had barely begun to fade before it was followed by others. Outside the bar, in the flowerbeds, tree frogs who inhabited the ornamental shrubbery began to serenade. They didn't seem to be bothered by the thunder. A stray dog, frightened by that same thunder, came into the bar and went somewhere behind it to hide. No one admonished the animal, such as might happen in the states, but welcomed him to a place where he felt safe.

The air began to smell of rain, and then it came. It was not a cloudburst, but a fairly heavy, steady patter on the deck-boards by the pool. It brought with it a feeling of peace and relaxation, which Angie immediately responded to, closed her eyes and welcomed.

Suddenly, a voice interrupted her reverie. It was Dimitri. "Are you a scuba diver?" he asked.

Angie had been enjoying the sounds and smell of the rain. Coming back from her own world, she turned toward him. "What? Oh, sure. Yes. Why do you ask?"

"Well, my crew was called away on another job. I was hoping to pick up somebody from here. Are you certified?"

At this point, Al jumped in. "Does a cat have climbing gear?" he found himself saying.

"Great," Dimitri said. "Come to work for me. The pay is very good, and the work is light."

Now Dimitri had Angie's full attention. "Describe "light work"," she said.

"Basically, be my support team. Help me get geared up to dive, that kind of thing. I'll need one of you to be my dive partner and one to act as crew to stay on the boat when I'm in the water."

Angie looked at Al. He nodded yes and smiled. "So, this means you're going to the Great Blue Hole?" she asked.

"Yes, I am. Bright and early in the morning," Dimitri said.

Angie extended her right hand to "shake on it." "Yeah, we'll be your crew. Absolutely. What all do we need to know? Oh—there's a third member in our party, a young man of fourteen. Can he join us?"

"Sure, no problem. Well, you pretty well already know most of it," he said with a smile. "If you're certified scuba divers, you know the gear, you know the routine. I have special tanks that are filled with mixed gas because I'm going to be swimming way back into those grottos. Uh, do you know anything about the Great Blue Hole?"

"We've been there," Angie said.

"There is a widely believed theory which says those grottos are part of an underwater labyrinth, a cavern network which extends not only to the mainland coast but continues most of the way underneath this country. If that's true, those divers might have gotten curious and gone cave-diving without the proper equipment. It would be very easy to get turned around and lost in there. At 150 feet, they didn't have much time, anyway. They would have run out of air within a few minutes. Being goofy from nitrogen narcosis wouldn't have helped, either."

"So, they drowned?" Al offered.

"Maybe," Dimitri said, shrugging and raising upturned palms.

"God, that would be a hell of a way to die," Angie added.

"There's worse ways," Dimitri added, almost by mistake. "Anyway, I'm going to want one of you to also wear tanks with mixed gas, and wait by the entrance to the grottos, holding onto a rope that is attached to me, while I go in. The rope is quite literally a life-line. I would tie it to a mineral formation, but that is hardly reliable."

"Hardly," Angie agreed.

"So, which one of you wants to be on the safety end of that rope?" Dimitri asked with a smile.

"I do," Angie said, without missing a beat. "But I've never used mixed gas before."

"I'll prep you on the way out there in the morning," Dimitri said. "By the time we get to the hole, you'll be an expert."

Everyone shook hands again and said they would meet in the morning. As Angie and Al walked away, she mumbled, mostly to herself, "Strange. That guy showed up in the nick of time."

Al heard but did not respond. He veered off to join James, who was sitting at a table on the edge of the deck, under an overhang and out of the rain. He was excited to fill him in on the next day's plans.

CHAPTER SIX

Incident at the Great Blue Hole

T he next morning, the fifty-foot yacht sped across crystal blue water toward Lighthouse Reef and the Great Blue Hole with Dimitri, Al, Angie, and James in the open stern.

Dimitri was briefing Angie on mixed-gas diving while Al walked from one side of the boat to the other, taking pictures of everything, including the sunrise. Since Scott wasn't there, he had taken it upon himself to photographically record the entire trip. Having no delusions about being as good a photographer as Scott, he thought he could still take some shots and have fun with it.

"There are a lot of misconceptions about mixed gas," Dimitri was saying. "It doesn't allow the diver to stay down longer, and you still have to follow the same protocol when surfacing; things like making all of the decompression stops. What it does do is prevent you from getting goofy from nitrogen narcosis. No hallucinations, no dizziness. You can think a lot clearer. And under the circumstances, that's a very important thing."

Angie was attentive and nodding in agreement as Dimitri spoke. She was happy to finally be doing something positive and, of course, Dimitri was her free pass to the great Blue Hole, which was supposed to be forbidden territory while the investigation was under way. Even after the investigation was completed, the hole would probably be closed to the general public, except under special circumstances and with expensive permits. Since becoming independent from Great Britain, Belize had learned a lot about the revenue to be gained from 'permits' for almost everything.

On the other hand, the tragedy at the Great Blue Hole was bound to spark a lot more interest and curiosity among divers, prompting a flurry of newcomers. So, she supposed a lot depended on the Belize government's greed. But she didn't need to think all that through, then. She needed to listen carefully to Dimitri while he was still prepping her for the dive.

His voice broke through her thoughts. "We're both going to be wearing double tanks, which are connected with a dual manifold. We also have special BCs that can hold the two tanks. The problem is, they're so heavy we won't put them on while we're on the boat. We'll toss them into the water, then jump in after them and put them on in the water. For about the first one hundred feet going down, you'll feel like you have an entire submarine on your back. Beyond that, it's not so bad.

"We need the extra gas, not only because we'll be down there for a longer time, but we'll need it for our decompression stops on the way back up. We'll also be wearing full face masks equipped with intercom systems. I'll need to show you how to equalize pressure with a full-face mask since you can't grab your nose and blow, like you're used to doing."

Dimitri continued giving Angie careful instructions on the equalization process with a full-face mask, followed by other fine points of the dive. By the time he had finished briefing her, the boat was entering Lighthouse Reef and negotiating its way through the coral heads leading to the Great Blue Hole.

While Angie had been receiving information on the dive, Al continued to look for special shots to take of the scenery around them. As he turned his attention to the activity on the boat, he saw that the best images were to be found in what was right in front of him. Watching Angie getting suited up and preparing to descend into the Great Blue Hole, he was struck by the expression on her face that he wanted to capture: her jaw was set with determination and a sense of destiny, while her eyes betrayed fear mixed with bravery.

James had also been looking at Angie as she prepared to dive. Clasping and unclasping his hands in frustration, he turned toward Dimitri. "What am I supposed to be doing while all of this is going on?"

Dimitri placed a hand on his shoulder. "You, young man, are going to suit up and stand by for emergencies. If something does go wrong down there, we'll need back up. It may not sound like an important job, but believe me, it is. Or you can change places with Angie, if you would prefer."

"Over my dead body," Angie said. "No offense, James, but I'm going down in that hole."

"So, how will I know if anything is wrong down there?" James asked.

"The intercom system has a speaker box right here." Dimitri pointed to an elaborate piece of electronic equipment that sat on a nearby shelf adjacent to the salon door. "Not only can you hear us, you can talk to us. Just use the microphone and hold down the 'press to talk' button. As a matter of fact, I'm depending on you to hear every word or nuance we utter. I also have a bang stick here for you. Do you know how to use one, if you have to?"

"Absolutely," James said.

Dimitri reached into a long, leather pouch and withdrew three bang sticks and then pulled out ammunition from another waterproof pouch. "Here," he said, as he handed the shotgun and shell to James. "Load that thing with care. And make damn sure the safety is on before you do anything."

Accepting the bang stick and ammo, James felt decidedly better about the role he was to play. "Yeah, okay. I can do that," he said, smiling.

Angie seemed to be relieved, also, albeit surprised, when Dimitri loaded the other two bang sticks with shotgun shells. At one point, he looked at her with a wry smile and said, "We don't know what's down there. I'm not going to wind up like that victim they found. You know how to use one of these things?"

"Yes," Angie replied. "I've used one before."

"Oh yeah? It's hard to imagine you with a bang stick. What did you use it on?"

"One of those hammerheads in the Blue Hole."

"Yep," James said, "she saved all of us that day. That shark was going to make tacos out of us until Angie put the whammy on him."

"Really?" Dimitri said with a smile. "I'm impressed. That's very good. I've got a lady warrior on my team. It couldn't be better."

"What do you mean by that?" Angie asked.

"She has no power over women."

"What? Wait—how do you know about that? Who are you?"

Dimitri looked her in the eye. "Do not worry, Angie. I was sent by a friend."

Angie stared back for a long moment. "I knew it the minute the canary died. So, can I trust you?"

"I just handed you a loaded bang stick, didn't I?"

Just as they cleared the last coral head and entered the Great Blue Hole, a Belize Coast Guard boat with several uniformed Coast Guardsmen on board, approached their yacht. A voice over a loudspeaker said, in a thick Belizian accent, "Hove to, and prepare to be boarded!"

The captain of the yacht killed the motors. The Coast Guard vessel moved to within a few inches of it and a uniformed officer stepped from his vessel onto theirs.

"This area is prohibited right now, except for personnel with proper creden-shals," the officer said.

"I am Dimitri Mykos. I was assigned to come here by your government. Didn't they notify you that I was coming?"

The officer looked him over carefully. "Do you have identification?"

"Sure." Dimitri turned and went below decks. He returned within moments and handed his papers to the officer.

Upon inspecting them, he nodded approvingly, "Sorry to boder you, Mr. Mykos. We've been told of your impending arrival. Do you have the coast guard channel on your radio?"

Dimitri nodded from the doorway to the lounge.

"Good," the officer said. "We would ask that you report any findings to us immediately."

"Of course."

The Coast Guard officer then pointed at Al, James, and Angie who were standing together in the stern.

"Who are dese oder peoples?"

"They are my crew," Dimitri said without hesitation.

The officer nodded curtly and saluted, then turned and stepped back onto his own craft, which was quickly put in reverse and backed away.

Angie smiled at the others. Her eyes bright. "All right. Let's go hunting."

The divers spent the next several minutes gearing up, pulling themselves into wet suits, getting a final brief on the full-face masks, and checking the tanks to make sure they were full.

When they were ready, Oscar, the Belizean deckhand, helped them toss the two BCs and double tanks into the water.

Angie shuffled over to Al, kissed him on the cheek, and squeezed his arm. "Be careful down there," Al said, with a smile.

Angie smiled back, but it was clear she was a little nervous. "Not to worry. If I see her, I'm gonna stick this bang stick up her ass and find out if *that* will kill her."

James went over to Angie and gave her a hug. "I'll be right by this intercom. So, keep talking so I know what's going on down there."

"I will," she said, patting his cheek.

Turning away, she filled her lungs and blew out a long breath, ready for business. She and Dimitri then dove into the water, swam to their BCs, and wriggled into them, attaching all of the straps and buckles that held them in place. After placing the stage two part of the regulator in their mouths, and checking to make sure they could breathe, Dimitri called to Oscar to pass them the bang sticks. Taking them securely in hand, the two of them were on their way. With a thumb's down, they held their purge valves high, expelled all of the air in their BCs, rolled over in the water and began their dive.

As on her previous trip here, Angie was amazed at the clarity of the water. As she descended with Dimitri, she felt like she was looking through air. It was again a little unnerving when they went over the precipice of the incline and into the hole, the sudden depth making her feel like she might fall.

Descending rather rapidly, Angie looked down and soon saw the same thermocline as on her previous trip. Going through that milky deep layer was not her favorite part of the dive. At ten feet thick going across the space, a diver had to swim through it without being able to see their hands in front of their face. For whatever time it took to get through the opaque water, they were vulnerable against attack from any creature that might be lurking.

To guard against that happening, Angie sped up as she descended into the white layer, to get through it as fast as possible. Emerging through it, she was relieved, in a strange way, even though the water was colder here, which creates the thermocline; and the light values decreased dramatically. Everything was illuminated in half light. Angie thought of it as being 'spooky.'

Just below them, then, were the damn grottos, their destination. Dimitri unsnapped a pocket on his BC and withdrew a white, nylon rope of considerable length. Angie hadn't noticed before, but one end of it was secured to his

BC. Unwinding the rope, he handed it to Angie, who nodded in acceptance.

"These grottos completely encircle this hole," Dimitri said over the intercom. "There's no way to know where the 'best' place to look might be. All we can do is pick a spot and go for it."

He saluted a goodbye to her, turned, and selected a wide enough opening between the gigantic mineral formations that would allow him to enter.

Slowly, carefully, Dimitri moved forward, deeper between the giant stalactites and stalagmites which, together, looked like a hideous set of teeth in a giant maw. They were actually limestone mineral formations created by droplets of water hundreds of thousands of years ago when this cave was above water and still had a ceiling. In the darkness, unseen by an uncaring world, the water droplets continued unabated for centuries, each drop adding miniscule calcium deposits onto ever growing evidence that even stone on this planet is alive enough to grow.

Then, more than one ice age came and went, and the earth's water level rose, turning this open-air cave into an underwater labyrinth. The gigantic ceiling became inundated with water, weakening it until it collapsed, exposing a cave, hidden for millions of years, to the daylight world, albeit light that was filtered by hundreds of feet of salt water.

Is it any wonder that the father of Maris, a sea creature, thought this place would be a secure sanctuary for his daughter? It was secluded, secreted deep within the confines of a reef. The hole, then unnamed as it was unknown by man, offered the safety of depth and the grottos offered security where she could abide in peace, have an unlimited food source, and make friends with some of the higher-intelligence sea creatures.

For nearly two thousand years, the siren lived in solitude and peace. Then came the advent of modern scuba diving equipment, and with it, adventurous people who wanted to brag that they had dived places where no one else had gone. But when one diver tells ten, at least five of that number has to keep up with the Joneses. And thus, it came to pass that the Great Blue Hole of Belize emerged as a prize spot for adventurous divers who wanted a special notch on their 'growing resume' of exotic places to dive.

It must have been that every time Maris, the siren, looked up, she found her lair being invaded by yet another diver—or worse, several divers at a time, for no diver dives alone. On a deep dive such as to the grottos of the Great Blue Hole, it is much safer to be in a group, in case of trouble. And then, most of those divers carried cameras so they could record their boldness and bravery. If she were to be seen, her picture would be taken and there would be photographic evidence of her existence.

Maris became fearful of exposure. All it would take is one diver seeing her and it would be on the evening news. Her existence would be in jeopardy. She envisioned a full color trophy photo on the cover of *The Saltwater Angler Magazine*; herself being the trophy.

She couldn't risk it. She finally decided to take action and hatched a plan, naïve though it was, whereby she would murder everyone aboard one of the dive boats that frequented the site. If an empty boat were to be found mysteriously floating atop the Great Blue Hole, it would create a stigma not unlike the one that tainted the Caribbean area known as the Bermuda Triangle, and people would avoid it. Her home would once again be solemn and secure. No more divers. No more trash drifting down, jettisoned by people on the surface who have no respect for the purity of this place.

Or so she thought. But Maris had little experience with the human mind or how it processed such events. It never occurred to her that the very opposite would happen. She knew not of the folly of human beings to rush toward danger, instead of running from it. And her first attempt to execute her plan was a miserable failure, thanks to a pissed-off ghost and a twelve-year-old boy. She had barely survived the wounds she received in that battle: two gunshot blasts to the chest, plus a knife in the back put there by the boat captain. Indeed, it had been a very close brush with death. Her survival had been nothing short of miraculous.

Her second attempt had been more successful. There had been no twelve-year-old kid on board this latest boat to arrive that would throw a monkey wrench into the works, and she was more prepared. She had learned things from her first encounter with humans.

That dive group's adventure to the grottos had been their last. But even that had backfired because now, there were boats all over the place, all of them filled with scientific men and women, intent on investigating the mysterious death and searching for the missing passengers; trying to find out what had gone wrong on this sport diving trip. Captain Gordon Hughes had predicted it would be this way. Maris had foolishly ignored his warning, believing that the old man was trying to run a bluff.

And there, too, she had failed miserably. It was her

second attempt to kill the wise old boat captain, and he had slipped the noose she was about to use to kill him. Just as she started to change into her alter being, the old man had plunged a knife into her back. The pain had been awful and numbing. She had lost all control long enough for Captain Gordon Hughes to push her away, scramble into his Zodiac and speed off. She had failed. But she had learned from the experience.

Now she was faced with another, more frightening dilemma, for she had no place to hide. She had to find another solution; one to quell this latest problem. But what? Her inexperience and naiveite were showing. And horribly, her inner sanctum was being invaded more than ever before. At this point, she was operating from fear, and that was not a good position to be in. It clouded her ability to reason.

———

Dimitri moved slowly and cautiously forward, deeper into the grotto, looking for any sign that intelligent life dwelled here. So far, everything looked exactly as it should look— large mineral formations hanging down, with others protruding upward from the floor of the shallow cavern. Sediment had accumulated over the ages and was settled on everything, making the white stone appear grayish brown. Just then, he heard Angie's voice over the diver-to-diver PA system.

"How does it look in there?"

"This is certainly not where I would want to hang out during my summer vacations," Dimitri responded. "Same ol', same ol', with the mineral formations. A few deep water spider crabs. Getting darker. I'm removing my flashlight from the BC pouch and attaching it to the bang stick with the Velcro strap. There! Turning on a light exposes a lot more of the true colors, but that still isn't saying a lot. Just lots of sediment in here. Any movement, no matter how slight, stirs it up." After a couple of more minutes, he added, "There's nothing here. I'm coming out."

As Dimitri was trying to turn around, he felt movement in the water move on his left side. He turned his head and was shocked to see a grotesque monster with huge tentacles and bulging eyes, with elliptical pupils staring straight at him from only a couple of feet away.

"The sto kalo!" Dimitri said, incredulously.

"What?" came Angie's voice over the PA.

Dimitri quickly swiveled the bang around so that it was pointing directly at the creature that seemed to recognize it as a danger and began quickly retreating, causing the water to become wavy. There was a blur where the creature had been. Then another form began to take shape. Maris, clad in a flimsy white dress, swam in front of him, looking relaxed, smiling at him.

Dimitri froze. He knew he must be hallucinating and should have taken aggressive action against this vision before him, for this was the siren! But it was the sound of sweet singing that put him in check. He was helpless. He could do nothing.

Suddenly, there was a strong tugging on the rope. He was being pulled backward by Angie. She must have heard the singing, too, and knew well what it was. However, being a woman, the siren song had no effect on her. Angie was now pulling on the rope harder than ever. Dimitri was being drawn out of the grotto, roughly, but safely.

"Dimitri, wake up," he heard Angie yelling. "That

singing you hear is the bitch siren, and she's trying to mesmerize you. If she succeeds, you'll never leave this place alive."

Dimitri slammed into a huge stalactite, and the impact helped to break the trance he was in. He slapped the side of his head to jar himself back to consciousness; and it worked. The siren was out of sight by now.

Dimitri managed to say, "Quit pulling on the safety line. I'm okay and on my way out."

Once Dimitri cleared the grotto, the two divers began to ascend.

"You saw her, didn't you?" Angie asked.

"Yes, I saw her. But I don't think she wanted to harm me."

"Don't be naïve. She would have had you for a Greek salad."

James was now yelling into the intercom, "Y'all all right down there?"

"Yes, we're on the way up," Angie said. "Dimitri just saw the siren. But she isn't following us. I think we're safe."

"I hope so," James said. "But I recommend keeping a sharp eye out. You can never tell with that broad."

"Will do," Angie replied.

————

Back at Robert's Grove, Angie took a long hot shower, then dressed in light clothing and walked out to the deck adjacent to the bar. Al, James, and Michael Longsworth, manager of Robert's Grove, were there, sitting at a table talking with Dimitri. Angie joined the group.

Ol' Jenkins was in his wheelchair at a table on the far side of the deck, a drink in front of him. He was babbling to nobody in particular. "Life ain't nothing but a fucking death sentence," he was saying. "Nobody understands that. From the moment you're born, it's just a countdown until you croak. You're gonna die. Don't matter how rich you are. Don't matter how famous you are. Don't matter how many diplomas you have, you're toast! Kaput! No mas, cabron! TIME! Time ain't nobody's friend. She takes no prisoners! Time is a merciless whore!"

After watching the old man for a minute, Angie turned to Michael and asked, "What's up with him?"

Michael slowly shook his head. "He gets like that sometimes. The scary part is, he makes a little too much sense. Says things out loud that most of us keep silent in thought."

"Well, shouldn't somebody do something about it?" Angie asked.

"Whatcha gonna do?" Michael responded, holding up his hands. "Am I supposed to kick him out? He's got nothing, no place to go. He lives in a little room, 'bout the size of a shoebox, back from the beach. He's in that chair because of the bends. His daughter was killed by sharks. He's got no one else. I guess it's kind of like having a dog in your house. If people don't like getting dog hair on their clothes, don't sit on the couch. If somebody doesn't like Ol' Jenkins ranting to himself, go to another bar. This is Belize, not the United States. Down here, we're a little more tolerant. 'The quality of mercy is not strained.' One hopeless, lonely old man drinks here for free. Let him have his reverie. He isn't hurting anybody."

Angie thought about Michael's words for a minute, and a smile formed on her lips. "You're a good soul, Michael."

"Thank you. I try to be. I try to think if it was me in that chair, how would I want to be treated? The Good Book says, Do unto others…"

"Well, that certainly brings me back to center," Angie said, smiling.

The waiter approached the table. "Some-ting cool to drink?"

Everybody, including Angie, ordered beer. James would have liked to but was offered a cool soda pop instead. "Don't be in such a rush," Al said to his son. "You'll have plenty of time to fuck up your life. The later start to get at it, all the better."

"It's just a beer, Dad," James protested.

"No, it's not," Al countered. "Conversation over."

When the beers came and things had settled down, Angie spoke in a hushed voice to Dimitri. "It seems clear to me that you're very familiar with the siren."

Dimitri gave a little shrug. "So?"

Angie twisted her mouth. "So…who are you? What is it that you are *really* doing here? It's time, as they say, to come clean."

Dimitri hesitated, then leaned forward in his chair to place his forearms against the table. "I told you. I was sent by a friend."

"What friend?"

"The old woman you met at the ranch."

"What?" Angie said.

Dimitri looked straight ahead, eyeing a young girl who was standing on the dock, looking out at the water.

"So, just what is it you're here to do?" Angie asked.

"It's very complicated," he answered. "But right now, I'm going to go check out that young chick on the dock."

With that, he pushed back his chair, got up and strode toward the dock and the young girl standing there, alone.

CHAPTER SEVEN

Search Over!

Hearing the distant sound of a chopper, Angie shaded her eyes with her hand to try to find it in the sky. It was a Coast Guard Medivac helicopter, a few miles offshore, apparently heading for Belize City. Just as it was fading out of sight, she spotted a second chopper that was headed straight toward Placencia. Moments later, it flew low over Robert's Grove and landed on the road behind the resort. Two men disembarked; then the chopper lifted off, and flew away, also toward Belize City.

The two men then walked into the reception area of the resort, registered at the desk, and headed for the bar. Angie observed all this as she was seated at a table with Michael, James and Al. Unable to contain her curiosity, she grabbed what was left of her beer, excused herself, and sauntered into the bar and walked over to the two new arrivals.

Smiling at the two men, she pushed her glass toward the bartender with a curt nod that she'd like a refill. Turning back to the men, she said, "That wasn't exactly a low-profile entrance. You been out at the Great Blue Hole?"

The taller of the two with a neat, well-trimmed beard, looked admiringly at the attractive young woman before answering, "Yes, ma'am."

"I'm Angie Holland, she said, extending her hand.

"Joe West," he said, shaking her hand.

The other man reached across and shook her hand, too. "Hugh Lipsey," he said with a smile.

"What's going on out there?" Angie asked. "They find anything else?"

"Yes, ma'am," Joe mumbled, looking down at his hands. "I'm afraid they did."

"What?" Angie asked, her eyes searching his face. "What?" she repeated when he didn't answer immediately.

Joe's voice was low when he responded. "They found the other missing bodies. All of them."

"Oh, Jesus," Angie said, sinking into a captain's chair. "Where were they?"

"The Coast Guard took a mini-sub down to the bottom of the hole. All of them were there... at least, what was left of them. They were scattered from one side of the hole to the other."

"What do you mean, 'what was left of them'?"

Joe hesitated a moment. "I mean, they were mutilated. It was horrible...gruesome. Nothing left from the neck up on any of them. Just scraps of flesh. It was soul-wrenching. What's left is being flown to a lab in Miami for autopsy."

Angie was quiet for several moments before asking, "What are your parts on all this?"

"We're catastrophic-event investigators. That was an American owned yacht, so the government assigned us to investigate. But today was just too damn upsetting, even for us. It was like being at a battle scene in a war. We decided to back off and try to refocus, get away from the site for a while."

"You got any theories?"

"Theories? No. Some people think it was sharks. But that just isn't so. The wounds were too uniform. Every one of them was basically the same." Joe shook his head. "Never seen anything like it. Hope I never do again. I'll have nightmares for years!"

"So, what was it?"

"I have no idea…no idea. No idea at all. What I do know is, there's something out there, intent on killing people. We thought maybe we would get some clue from satellite images. But there's nothing there, either."

"What do you mean satellite images?"

Joe pointed up. "There are satellites floating around up there with cameras that can pick up a tick on a dog. But they didn't show anything. We saw the divers go in the water. They went down. But then, they never came back up. The fact is, we may never know the truth."

"What?" Angie asked. "Why?"

"Don't you know? There are 'many' mysteries that have happened at sea, starting with the Devil's Triangle. The first reported anomaly there was written about by Christopher Columbus, who claimed he saw a giant ball of fire fall into the water. Might have been a meteor; who knows? But since then, there have been hundreds of planes and ships that have just disappeared in that area. Most people have heard about the Lost Squadron of Avenger airplanes that disappeared. What isn't well known is that they sent out a search plane to look for the avengers with thirteen crew members on board, and it also disappeared. Poof! Just disappeared. None of the planes have ever been found to this day, even with modern sonar and sub-sea search equipment. My point is, Ms. Holland, genuine mysteries *do* exist, like it or not."

Angie didn't ask any more questions. She stared at the bar and felt like she couldn't get her breath. Emptying her beer glass, she set it down and said to the bartender, "Give me something stronger."

When he obliged her, she slid out of her chair, mumbled something to Joe West about it being nice meeting him, then walked back outside as if in a trance, carrying her drink. She staggered slightly, not from alcohol, but from the vision of seven divers dying, being confronted by the worst nightmare imaginable moments before meeting their death. And for what?

What a horrible death it had to have been. And then there was the conflict. She was one of the few people on earth who knew what had really happened down there, but she couldn't tell anyone, because they would think she was mentally unbalanced—like Ol'Jenkins sitting over there in his wheelchair, babbling to himself.

The old woman who had mysteriously appeared to her and James at the ranch had been no help. Angie had discounted her 'formula' to kill the siren. 'Say a prayer to the star group Argo, and then allow yourself to be killed by the siren.' What the hell was that? It'll kill her, but you'll never know, because you'll be dead! Sheesh!

Her glass was empty again. Odd. She didn't remember finishing it, but she must have because the bartender had just walked up with a fresh drink. It made her wonder who around her knew what? Did all of these people know about the siren, but were keeping it to themselves because they also did not want to chance being hauled away in the white ambulance?

Why couldn't James's bang stick have just done the job and none of this would be necessary? Angie began to feel herself shut down; to want to isolate herself from other people. She had always been a natural-born problem solver. It was her nature. It was her instinct. But now she was faced with a dilemma that seemingly did not have a logical solution, and people's lives were at stake. Al's voice beside her pulled her out of her musings.

"I've never seen you this tied up in knots. You're tuning everybody out, Angie."

"I don't know what anybody can do to help. I don't even know what to do, or where to begin. Do you know how frustrating that is? I *have to do* something. Lives depend on it. And...here I am, stuck in neutral. The clock is ticking. That evil monster is plotting her next attack, right now, as we speak. And I don't know what in the living, breathing hell to do about it."

Al put a hand on her shoulder as she stood at the deck railing. "Lighten up on yourself. If you make yourself sick with worry, you aren't going to be of any use to anybody, not even yourself. And like you've said, a lot is riding on this." He retrieved his camera he was carrying on his back on a shoulder lanyard and took her picture.

"What did you do that for?" she asked.

"Documentation. I want to show you what you look like," Al replied, and turned the camera so Angie could see the playback screen.

Angie glanced at the image, but she was more interested in watching Dimitri less than a hundred yards away making out with the girl on the dock near several boats that were moored there. "Who is that young, split-tail girl that Dimitri is hitting on?"

Al glanced over to where Angie was looking. "Oh, her. I met her yesterday. She came up behind me while I was fishing. Said her name is Mara, or something like that."

"Mara?" Angie said, her eyes widening. "Isn't that just a little bit too close to 'Maris'?"

"I thought about that, but this kid is super young. Probably a millennial. Practically a teenybopper."

"Teenybopper? Jesus Christ, Al, what decade are you from?"

Al held up two fingers to make a 'V'. "Hey, peace, man!"

Angie laughed. Al had managed to lift her from her dark mood, at least for the moment. "Heaven help us! I suppose you went to Woodstock too."

"Yep, but I didn't stay long. It started raining. Things got muddy. Crosby, Stills, Nash and Young were on stage. They said something like, 'Fuck it. We'll come back after the rain stops.' I thought it was the most sensible thing I had heard all day. Besides, there was pot everywhere. The air was filled with it. I never did get into that kind of stuff. To me, it always smelled like the leaves I used to rake into a pile and burn during the fall when I was a kid."

"Be careful," Angie said aloud to herself. "We've been infiltrated by a square."

"Oh no. Don't tell me you're a pot smoker?"

Angie shook her head. "No. Not now. But when I was in college, I tried it. What stopped me was, I had a dear friend, Regina Goodman, who also tried it. She got hooked and then moved up to other stuff. The marijuana was a gateway drug. I saw her life going right down the tube. Here was this woman who had all the potential in the world to be a lawyer, a political leader, somebody important. Instead, she wound up dead. I can't think of any 'good time' that is a good enough time to be worth that."

"I should say not," Al agreed.

Angie was still watching Dimitri make out with the girl. Now they were moving away from the dock, toward the bar. "Oh shit," Angie thought. "He's going to ply her with alcohol and then teach her how to make love 'the Greek way'!" She felt a rush of jealousy. She didn't understand why, but there it was.

Dimitri and the girl were within a few feet of Angie on their way to the bar. He winked at her as they passed. Angie looked back at him, not sure what her expression conveyed. As the couple walked by, she closely observed the young girl, 'Mara'. Was that her name? Could that possibly be a form of 'Maris'? The girl certainly didn't look threatening. Maybe it was just a coincidence. After all, wasn't 'Mara' a popular name for millennials?

Staring after the attractive girl, she thought—little bitch. She looked so young. Angie had believed Dimitri was sophisticated enough to not be drawn in by that kind of uncooked bread. What could she have that Angie didn't have? And why, Angie thought, was she having such thoughts? After all, she was in a committed relationship with Scott. She had been for several years, and she had never felt any desire to, to, to…shit! She didn't even want to think about it. Still, when she looked at Dimitri, there was no denying a wetness in her crotch.

Suddenly, the waiter was standing beside her, a white bar towel folded over his arm. "Your drink okay, ma'am?"

Angie looked at her glass, then drained it. Handing it to

the bartender, she said, "No, as a matter of fact, I need another one, please."

"Yes, ma'am, right away."

It was a beautiful day in Placencia. Angie wished she could be worry free and enjoy it. Damn that siren, anyway... ruthless killer that she was.

CHAPTER EIGHT

What Are these Strange Feelings?

A ngie woke up with a terrible hangover the next morning. She grabbed at her head with both hands and moaned.

"Augh! Sonofabitch! What do they put in that Siren's Potion?" She sat up on the side of the bed and tried to stand up, but her first attempt failed. She plopped back down, still holding her head, moaning, and mumbling something about 'never again.'

"I haven't been this smashed since college graduation. Why did I do it to myself?"

She made a second, more successful attempt to stand up, but she wobbled as she headed for the bathroom. She reached the toilet just in time. Much of the Siren's Potion came back up and filled the toilet. Angie held her hair back with one hand and braced herself with the other as she purged. The sounds she made, and the smell were both repugnant. In between salvos, she cursed herself, the world in general, and Harold, the bartender, for taking her so literally.

An hour later, she made her way to the restaurant, looking somewhat put together, albeit her skin color was pale and her eyes were bloodshot. She found a table and sat down as gently as possible, so as not to jar her system, or her head.

The waiter came to her table, bearing hot coffee and a plate of pan dulce, which he placed before her with the greeting, "Good morning, mum."

"Good morning," Angie answered without looking up. To do so was painful. "Thank you. Just leave me with this. That's about all I can handle for now."

The waiter retreated. Angie took a careful sip of the hot coffee and placed a piece of the pan dulce on a saucer. Picking it up, she took a bite of the fresh, sweet bread. It tasted good, but she would probably enjoy it more if her head wasn't throbbing like jungle drums.

After she had taken a few deep breaths and sips of coffee, she sensed movement alongside of her and saw that it was Dimitri. "Good morning!" he chirped. "Mind if I join you?"

"Sure," Angie agreed. "Maybe a little distraction will take my mind off of this pain."

"Oh? Got blasted last night, did we?" Dimitri said with a smile as he seated himself.

"Blasted? I got blown clear out of the water."

"And now you're paying the price."

The waiter arrived at the table with coffee and pan dulce for Dimitri. Holding up an index finger, he asked, "Could you please bring us two bowls of diced, mixed fruit?"

"Yes, suh. Right away," he replied, then retreated toward the kitchen.

Dimitri turned toward Angie. "The natural sugars in the fruit will help dull the blade a little. It's not a cure, but it'll help."

"Good to know," Angie said. "So, how did your chance meeting go last night?"

"Pretty much as expected."

"Oh? Is she an 'almost' virgin teenybopper, or a rapacious slut? My money is on rapacious slut."

"I'd have to guess somewhere in the middle," he said as he bit into a piece of pan dulce.

"So, you did bang her brains out, as I suspected," she ventured, taking another sip of coffee.

"Something like that," Dimitri answered. Putting down his bread, he looked questioningly at her. "What's going on here? What difference does it make what I did with some split-tail girl?"

Angie waved away his rebuke. "Oh, no. You're right. It's none of my business. It's this unbelievable hangover. I'm not speaking rationally. I'm sorry."

The waiter arrived with two bowls of diced fruit — mango, papaya, cantaloupe, peach, and avocado. There were key limes, cut in half, on an accompanying plate, meant for squeezing on the fruit, which Dimitri did for both of them.

"Dig in," he said. "You'll feel better in no time." Angie grabbed her fork and speared a piece of mango. As she chewed, she said, "So, where is the little miss this morning?"

"Dunno. When I woke up, she was gone."

"Gone?"

"Yep, just...gone! No kiss, no goodbye—just gone. Almost made me feel guilty that I hadn't left any money on the dresser."

That made Angie smile. "Okay," she managed between

bites of fruit that were hitting the spot. "Let's cut through the bullshit for a minute, okay? Who the fuck are you, *really*? And who the fuck is she, *really*? And what the fuck is going on here, *really*? I know damn well you didn't come all the way to Belize just to get your ashes hauled. And I don't believe working for the government of Belize is anything more than a cover. You've got too much going on for the game to be that simple. I see shit going on around me that on the surface looks simple enough. And it looks like everybody is playing their own game. But something tells me none of this is simple. I think we've all been called here by some common force to work *as a team* to accomplish one goal. Am I right, or am I imagining things?"

Dimitri munched fruit from his bowl for a long minute, seeming to not have heard her. But then he paused, wiped his mouth with the cloth napkin and said softly, "Of course you are right. But don't say it too loud. You never know who might be listening."

Angie looked around. "Who? We're the only ones here."

"Yes, right now we are. But make it a habit. You never know who might walk up behind you."

"Okay. I can deal with that. But let's start with my first question. Who the fuck are you, 'really'?"

"I'm here to break the siren's heart, and therefore, her spirit."

"What? Now you've...what the hell are you talking about?"

"In order for the siren to be killed, she must be distressed. She must be heart-broken and see no purpose in going on. That is what will weaken her."

"Soooo, I was right! There is some kind of a 'formula' as such, that will lower the shields around her."

"That's very astute of you, Angie. You know that much, so that's a good start. But you also need to know this: the 'formula,' as you put it, must be followed exactly, or it will be ineffective."

"Jesus! Is there anything that can make this any more complicated than it already is? Who sent you?"

"The old woman you met at the ranch. Her name is Minerva."

"The old woman." Angie stared into space as she thought back. It was two days ago, and yet it seemed like eons ago. "Okay, just for clarification, why would you be chosen as the one she falls in love with?"

"Her heritage is Greek. Her mother comes from the island of Sirenuse, off the coast of Italy, but yet, her heritage is Greek. That's why the Greeks first wrote of the three sirens."

"The bitch has been around for nearly two thousand years. How are you supposed to make her fall in love with you?"

"By removing her from her natural element. Any time she copulates, it is either in the water or over the water, such as, on a ship, a boat, an oil platform. But if she is removed from the water, even as much as fifty feet, she becomes vulnerable to human emotions. All of her natural defenses are lowered."

"No shit? And how do you know this?"

"Minerva."

Angie was silent for a couple minutes while she thought about his words. "So, why am I here? What is my part in all this?"

"You are, let's say, the director of the play— this Greek tragedy. You are the coordinator, the producer. You are here to make sure all of the players are in the right place at the right time."

Angie was suddenly sober. Her eyes widened. "Well, I'm glad somebody let me in on this little bit of news! To me, it sounds like I'm a pivotal player. Don't you think it might have been helpful if I had been told sooner?"

"Been told what sooner?" Al Harmon asked, as he walked up to the table with James. After greeting the others, they each grabbed a chair and sat.

Angie put down her fork. "You both need to know, but it's a little bit complicated and I have a headache." She glanced at Dimitri. "Would you mind?"

"Sure," Dimitri said with a nod. Leaning over the table, he spoke in a low voice, repeating what he had just told Angie, while glancing around the whole time he was speaking. "We can't let anyone overhear this," he explained. "Particularly that young girl you met, Al, who calls herself Mara."

After he finished telling them of the complicated plot to weaken and destroy the siren, Angie asked, "Okay, what's next? Do we just wait for you to drill the girl's brains out? For that matter, do you think that Mara is Maris—one morphed as the other person?"

Dimitri nodded. "I'm pretty sure of it. Actually, almost certain."

How can you be so sure?" Angie persisted.

"When I asked her where she was from, she said, 'Daytona Beach, California'."

Angie raised an eyebrow. "While it's clear she's lying, that's not proof. Unfortunately, few millennials are members of Mensa. I've had a couple encounters with them regarding simple math, like making change when I bought something at a burger joint or a dollar store. It's sad, really, and speaks volumes about the inadequacy of our educational system in America."

Dimitri put his hand on her arm. "Stay on track. Mara is no millennial. That is, 'if' she is who I think she is. She's just spent most of her life underwater."

"Yeah," Angie said. "Isn't that pretty much the same thing? Never mind. Let's run with your assumption for now. Okay, so Mara is Maris in drag. Go do your thing, Dimitri. Capture the heart of this blood thirsty, rapacious killer vamp, so we can put the whammy on her. All we need now is some sucker willing to put his life on the line, and just about everything will be in place."

"No, that isn't quite 'all.' You are also going to need an executioner, a person to plunge a knife in her at precisely the right moment. And that person has to be below the age of puberty. In her final moments, she will probably call on that which she knows so well as a way to neutralize the enemies who surround her."

———

"I don't think we have much choice," he said. "I regret having to do it. I had hoped to keep the little tyke separate from some of the Harmon legacy. But...he is a Harmon. I'll make sure his mother is ready to bring him when the moment is right."

"Good," Dimitri said. "Meanwhile, I would advise any of you, including myself, to act as normal as possible when Mara presents herself, so she won't smell a rat. Or...in her case, a dead fish."

Al got a curious look on his face. "So, we're just

supposed to kick back while Dimitri here gets as much trim as possible?"

"That's about the size of it," Angie said.

"Well, I hope 'the size of it' is big enough to keep that whore happy." Al gestured toward Dimitri.

Without a word, Dimitri stood up and unbuckled his pants, then dropped his laundry down to his knees, exposing himself to everyone at the table. They stared for a long moment before he pulled up his pants.

"Okay," Al said. "I damn sure won't worry about that anymore! Dimitri, do me a favor. Don't come to Texas. I do *not* want my wife to meet you."

"Or my girlfriend," James said.

"You don't have a girlfriend," Al said, looking at his son.

"Are you forgetting about Athena?" James replied.

"Oh yeah," Al said. "You still going with her? I thought you two broke up."

"Nah, we made up. You know that no woman can resist a Harmon!"

"Heaven help us," Al said.

Angie was staring into space. "I must be hallucinating," she said, breathlessly after a minute.

"Oh no. You saw the same thing we all did," James said with a wide grin. "This Greek is hung like a Georgia mule!"

Al slapped James on the arm. "James, where did you learn to talk like that?"

"From listening to you, Dad."

Just then, the waiter appeared at the table. "Would anyone like anything else for breakfast?" he asked.

"Yeah, sausage and eggs," Angie answered.

CHAPTER NINE

Let's Get Serious

Angie found that Dimitri was right when he said she was the "director" in this life-and-death play. For the next several days, she meticulously laid out a scenario for Maris's death. It felt bizarre, even when she tried to rationalize it, knowing that it had to happen. "I'm plotting a murder," she said to herself. "And it feels so natural—like some kind of a board game called Kill the Siren. Am I a female Jack the Ripper?"

Meanwhile, investigators were running around like monkeys at a circus, looking for 'the truth' behind the deaths at the Great Blue Hole. Special dive equipment was being brought in from Virginia, along with several deep-water experts.

Calling them experts had confirmed to Angie what her father had said on the subject. "Don't be impressed by somebody who is called an 'expert' at anything, honey," he'd told her. "The only thing an 'expert' is, is somebody with a little bit of knowledge a long way from home." And here was the proof. Angie found herself surrounded by idiots, pontificating on a plethora of theories, all of which made about as much sense as geese flying backwards. They had zero idea what they were doing and spent most of their waking hours trying to keep that fact a secret—even from themselves. No need to go to the circus. It was already here!

Robert's Grove Resort was booked solid with these so-called experts. At night, they filled the bar with their presence and filled the air with their crazy ideas. Angie saw them, heard them, but couldn't tell you a word they said because she had tuned them out. Her attention was riveted on Dimitri as she saw him come and go with 'Mara.' Imagining his activities with the woman took up more of her attention by the day. She tried not to think so much about the handsome, well hung Greek stud, but there it was, like a bug flying around in her mind that would not leave her alone.

She had not heard from Scott since he departed Placencia; but at this point, she didn't really care. What she wanted to do was to justify in her mind and heart having a love tryst with Dimitri. He may have been putting moves on Mara, but he was invading Angie's heart without trying or even knowing about it. It eventually reached the point where she could think about little else, which is not what she wanted to do. She felt her thoughts about him verged on obsession, and she didn't understand why. It had never happened before, and God knows, she had met enough handsome men in her business dealings.

It reached the point where there were two plans. First, of course, was the plan to kill the siren. But then, there was a parallel plan—*her* plan—to make Dimitri desire her as much as she desired him.

Through it all, she was confused about why she was obsessed with the idea of intimacy with Dimitri. She had never felt this kind of intense emotion before. Even her affair with Scott, leading up to their live-in relationship, had never involved the strong feelings she was experiencing now. And at this point, there had been no physical contact with Dimitri to affirm her feelings. She had a premonition that such an encounter was coming, because there's an old reliable saying that "Where the mind goes, the ass must follow".

Her relationship with Scott had seemed so practical. He was an artist, but a miserable failure as a businessperson, which is not uncommon among true artists. Angie was a businesswoman. She had a logic that appealed to other businesspeople. Together, they made a good fit. A team, if you will.

He needed a representative to present his work to the world. She needed a product to sell that was exclusively hers. A little hanky-panky on the side was topping on the dessert, a sweet syrup on the bread pudding. It was nice. It was comfortable. But it was never intense. She had never stayed awake at night wondering what it would be like to have Scott inside of her. With Dimitri, she couldn't think of anything else. It was maddening. She didn't like it. It was driving her buggy, and try as she might, she could not figure out why.

Sure, Dimitri was hung like a circus elephant, and that was an eye opener, to say nothing of a leg opener—but that wasn't all. There was the way he looked at her with that sideways smile when he was amused. Those eyes. Those goddamned chocolate brown eyes. They looked right into her without trying. She wondered how much Dimitri knew about her, just by looking at her. Did he see her desire for him? Was he intentionally toying with her, waiting for just the right moment, before he graced her with that giant schlong of his? Oh, God! What was it going to feel like when he invaded her with that thing? When? She had just said 'when', not 'if'. That meant that in her mind, it was a done deal—a plan, a conspiracy on her part to seduce the seducer. Oh, Geez! She was turning into a wanton slut. Or had she been one all along, and never knew it? Were all women wanton sluts under the right conditions?

"Hi, I'm Angie, the wet pussy vamp, just waiting to wrap my legs around you and squeeze you like a Valencia orange until I've drained all of the juice out of you." Angie rolled her eyes upward. She had the fever. Maybe a walk would help.

She rose from the table and walked toward the beach, repeating the words, "Blue sky—blue sky—blue sky." in her head, over and over again to prevent any other thoughts from forming. She was tired of thinking about Dimitri and his huge, delicious-looking popsicle. She shook her head as though to clear her mind. To hell with all of it. A walk would do her good, help clear her mind and loosen up her muscles, which right then seemed to be tied in knots.

Angie had walked along the beach for about a half hour when she spotted an old pier that spiked off the beach, jutting into the water for a hundred yards or so. The structure looked rather picturesque and thought that if Scott were here, he would capture the image, for sure. The weathered pier seemed somehow 'lonely'. After studying it for a minute or more, Angie decided to walk out on it so she could look down into the clear water at the end of it and see what fish might be swimming around.

She should have sensed danger the minute she set foot onto the first plank and it creaked under her weight. Pier planks are not supposed to 'creak' when you walk on them.

But perhaps she had been mistaken; maybe she had only thought she heard that sound because she had her mind on something else. But the warnings continued as she walked further out on the rickety dock. More planks definitely creaked, and she noticed the entire structure rocked slightly from side to side.

By the time she realized that the pier was unsafe, she had gone about a third of the way to the end. She turned around to come back, but it was too late. One of the old planks snapped in the middle when she put her weight on it and she fell through, letting out a scream as she did, and landing on her back on a cross brace beneath the pier. The pain was instant and so intense that she almost blacked out. Seeing stars, she dropped forward into the water, but remained aware enough to pull her head up to allow her to breathe.

But the pain was incredible. All she could do was hold onto one of the pilings and rest. For the next several moments, any movement was out of the question. Then, as if an angel had come to save her, she heard a voice off in the distance that gave her hope.

"Angie, is that you in the water?" It was James Harmon.

She tried to cry out, but a soft, "Yes, it's me," was all she could manage.

James didn't need to hear her voice, as he instinctively knew it was her. He had been walking down the beach, purposely following her at a distance to make sure she was safe. He ran into the water alongside of the pier to a depth where he needed to swim, yelling as he made his way toward her, "Hang on Angie! I'm on the way! Oh, shit, shit, shit!" He dived forward and swam as fast as he could.

Within moments, he reached her and freed her from the

piling, so she could slip her arms around his neck. "Where are you hurt?" he asked.

"Back," Angie replied through clenched teeth.

James turned over and, with Angie on his chest, he began to swim the backstroke heading toward shore.

Nearby, a young boy was walking down the beach, doodling with his cell phone. Hearing James talking to Angie, he looked up to see them when they were about waist deep in the water. Running into the surf, holding his phone up in one hand, he helped James pull Angie ashore. The two boys gently placed her on her back at the edge of the water.

"You got the number for Robert's Grove on that thing?" James asked.

"Yah, mahn."

"Good, please call them and tell them a guest is injured. They need to call the medics and get an ambulance down here, pronto."

Without a word, the boy hit the appropriate buttons on the phone. When Michael answered, the boy handed the phone to James.

"Who's this? Michael? James Harmon here. Angie has been hurt. We're on the beach a mile or so south of the resort. We need medics and a meat wagon...Shit! I mean, an ambulance down here. What? Yeah, an ambulance, something...Okay."

James handed the phone back. "Thanks," he said.

Within a couple of minutes, they heard a siren in the distance. The boy's phone rang. He answered, listened for a minute, then handed the phone to James again.

"Yeah? I don't know, we're by a pier." James put Michael on speaker.

Michael's voice was heard saying, "James, you're on the

coast. Saying you are by a pier is like saying you found a flea on a dog. Which pier?"

"I don't know. It's off by itself, kind of an old looking one with warped boards. That's how Angie got hurt. She fell through."

"Okay, I know which one," Michael said. "We'll be there in a minute."

The sound of sirens got louder, and then James saw the Robert's Grove van, closely followed by a white ambulance. The vehicles turned off the sand road onto the narrow beach, heading toward them. The van stopped a scant ten feet away, with the ambulance immediately behind him. Two medics got out of the ambulance and rushed toward James and Angie and the boy.

"What happened?" Michael wanted to know.

James pointed at the pier. "She apparently decided to take a walk on that old pier. One of the cross planks gave way, and she went through."

"I hit something on my way down," Angie managed to say through her pain. "I think it was one of those braces."

One of the medics was already hooking her up to a blood pressure cuff. The other returned to the ambulance for a stretcher. "Are you having any trouble breathing?" the attending medic asked.

Angie shook her head.

"Can you wiggle your toes?" he asked. Angie wiggled her toes in response, without a problem.

The second medic returned with the stretcher and the two men carefully lifted her onto it. "Okay, we going to take you to the clinic, now," the medic advised.

"Like hell you are. I'll be okay. Just take me to my room

at the resort. I hate clinics and hospitals. No. Make that, I *loathe* them."

"But you might have a back injury, or broken ribs," the medic protested.

"I'll take my chances," Angie said. "You try to take me to that clinic and I'll refuse to get into the ambulance."

The medics looked at Michael. "Take her to the resort," he ordered. "I'll call the doctor and get him to come to her room to examine her."

"But she's probably going to need x-rays."

"We'll cross that bridge when we come to it," Michael said with resignation. "Either of you two ever come up against a determined woman before?"

Both men nodded *yes*.

"Well then," Michael said, knowingly.

With Angie boarded into the ambulance, the vehicle made slow-progress through the sand, back up to the paved road. From there, it was only a few minutes' drive to Robert's Grove. Michael had called his friend, Dr. Evaristo Dominguez, and explained the situation.

A few minutes later, the good doctor pulled into the resort's parking lot just as the ambulance was arriving. A uniformed nurse accompanied him.

The doctor got out of his car carrying an old-fashioned black medical bag that was typical for physicians in Belize. Since so many people in Central America lacked transportation, or were located offshore on small cays, a doctor spent almost as much time in a car, or an island-jumper airplane, as he did in an office.

Dr. Dominquez flanked the stretcher as the medics wheeled Angie into her room. "How bad is the pain?" the doctor wanted to know.

"Compared to what?" Angie replied.

The doctor missed the sarcasm. "On a scale from one to ten?"

"A six, maybe seven."

Dr. Dominguez raised his brows. "That's pretty high up there."

After the medics had settled Angie in bed, the doctor began his exam in earnest. At one point, he carefully rolled her onto her stomach and gently ran his hands over her rib cage, then her spine.

"I just can't tell for sure," he said, shaking his head. "It doesn't feel like anything is broken, but I really need x-rays."

"No," Angie declared firmly.

Dimitri, who had entered the room and stood quietly to the side for a minute or so, spoke up. "Let me talk to her alone, Doctor. She'll be at the clinic a little later," he said with certainty.

The doctor turned to look at him. "Okay, I'll take your word for that," he said with a shrug. "There isn't a lot more I can do here, anyway, except maybe offer something for pain." He turned back to Angie. "But I'm not sure knocking you out is the right solution."

"I know some massage techniques that I learned in Greece," Dimitri offered. "With your permission, I would like to try those on her before she gets zonked with pills. I think I can relieve some of the pain."

The doctor started putting his instruments back in his bag. "Well, that seems a little unusual…but okay. If it seems to hurt her, stop immediately."

"Absolutely," Dimitri agreed.

As the doctor left the room with one of the medics, he said, more to himself, "I've never agreed to anything like that. I don't know why I did this time. Something about that guy…"

Dimitri looked at Michael and tilted his head toward the door for him to leave. When Angie and Dimitri were alone, he locked the door and closed the curtain. Coming back to her, he placed his hands on her back. "This is going to hurt for just the briefest moment," he said, gently. "Then your pain will begin to evaporate."

"How do you know?"

"Trust me. I've done this many times."

True to his word, his first touch sent shock waves up and down Angie's back, causing her to flinch and cry out. But then her pain started to dissipate. She couldn't believe it. It was as if it was simply draining away. Within three minutes of Dimitri moving his hands up and down her back, almost all of the pain had dissipated. She was in awe. It hadn't seemed as if he had actually applied any pressure or massaged the muscles. He had just touched her, tenderly, but thoroughly.

"What did you do?" she asked breathlessly.

Dimitri ignored her question. "What you did was very reckless. You need to take care. It isn't like you are a tourist here on vacation. You are vital to this mission. Without you, the whole thing never comes to fruition."

"What? What do you mean?"

"You are the director, the coordinator. You are the mortal that coordinates the actions of all the other mortals."

Angie blinked. "Before you go any farther, I want you to do one more thing for me, and then I need to know what you are talking about."

Dimitri smiled. "Yes, I will admit I want you too, but we need to have an understanding. This can happen only once. Afterwards, we will never speak of it again, nor repeat it."

"Agreed," Angie heard herself saying as she began unbuttoning her wet blouse. Moments later, she found herself standing nude in front of this Greek who spoke with an accent and referred to her as a 'Mortal', while at the same time being built like a Greek God. He disrobed, approached her, laid her gently on the bed, then lay down beside her. She looked into his eyes and felt a hunger unlike anything she had ever known before. She needed to taste those lips. She reached up put her arm around his neck and pulled his mouth to hers.

She had no idea how long the kiss lasted, but when that first one was over, she was dizzier than when she fell through the pier. That first kiss was immediately followed by a second. Dimitri's tongue searched deep inside her mouth. She welcomed it and sucked on it as if it were another part of his anatomy.

But it was Dimitri who first offered that special gift. He began licking Angie's chest and nipples, then worked his way down, across her belly, and stopped there to tease and delight her belly button with the tip of his tongue, which was a promise of things to come. He did not disappoint. When he reached her clitoris and sucked it gently into his mouth to manipulate it with his tongue, Angie had her first orgasm. It was intense, but she wanted more. At some point, positions were reversed, and it was Angie who took Dimitri deep in her mouth. The problem was, he was so big she had difficulty taking him as deeply as she wanted. But, as inspired as she was, she tried as hard as she could.

It was clear that Dimitri was in charge and he made sure foreplay lasted a very long time. There was no way he was going to short-change Angie, or himself, by rushing. By the time the moment arrived when he mounted Angie and entered her, she was beyond herself with desire, quivering, and pulling him toward her in spite of his size, to absorb even more of him. She wanted desperately to feel his pubic area rub against hers. But he was so large, she didn't think it was possible. Eventually, after repeated thrusts, she did take all of him. By that time, her eyes were wide with the overwhelming feeling of being completely filled like never before in her life.

He rode her this way without stopping to rest for well over an hour. By the time he did stop and pulled out, Angie was flooded, and also delighted. The room was filled with the pungent aroma of love musk that lingered as olfactory evidence that their love making had been intense.

After a few minutes, allowing time for both of them to recover, Dimitri pulled Angie into the shower, where he helped wash her from the top of her head to her feet. This bath was nothing short of a continuation of their love making, for even here, his touch was sensual. What was it about this Greek man that reeked so completely of sexual lust?

Later, Angie sat on the side of the bed, a towel wrapped around her, using another towel to dry her long, dark hair. Dimitri had put his pants on and sat bare chested in a chair across from her.

"The time has come for us to have a heart to heart," he said.

Angie quit drying her hair and looked at him, waiting.

"You are in the middle of something you do not completely understand because you have not been given the benefit of all the facts."

"What do you mean?" Angie asked.

Dimitri smiled a knowing, half-smile. "You know, modern humans think things like Atlantis never really existed. There is geological evidence which shows that islands appear from the sea, while others sink beneath the sea, almost daily."

Angie thought about his words, but she still wasn't connecting the dots. "Okay... so, what does that have to do with the price of tea in China?"

"Modern man passes off 'mythology' as the fantasy of some very inventive Greeks from a long time ago. I guess it's just easier for you that way. If you don't comprehend something, write it off as myth. You attach no possibility to the chance that some of those people might have really existed and were not just in the minds of writers such as Homer and Aesop."

Angie's eyes narrowed. "What are you saying? I'm beginning to think I know, but I want to hear it from your lips."

"I'm saying that you have awakened the minds and hearts of some very ancient people. Your pure heart and desire to save human lives has brought them, through time, to your aid. You are dead-on in your assumption that Maris is responsible for killing those people. We have been watching you and know that your goal is morally the right one. However, we also feel that you need guidance, so that you progress in the right direction to accomplish what needs to be done."

"Which is?"

"To kill the siren, of course. Truth be told, she should never have been born. But Leucosia was a trollop. All of the sirens were. But she was the most wanton vamp, the most lascivious. She wasn't happy with simply mating with humans. She went out and coupled with a hideous sea monster named Gonak. That was bad enough, but he knocked her up, and she had the child."

"Maris."

"Precisely. And, as it has turned out, she lived for nearly two thousand years before she got paranoid and went on a killing spree. She should have been killed hundreds of years ago. But she is resilient. I'll give her that."

"So...why are you here?"

"To help you kill her. It's going to take a team effort. Some of the players are in place, some are not. As the director, you've got to get them assembled, so they will all be in the right place at the right time."

"Okay, I believe that. But who are *you*, *really*? And who else is included when you say *we*?"

"The old woman you met at the ranch house isn't really an ugly old crone. She is beautiful and the wisest of the Greek Goddesses. She was in disguise so you could accept her easier."

"Okay?"

"Minerva is her true name."

"Minerva? The Greek goddess of wisdom? That Minerva?"

"The same, yes."

"So, you're telling me that I am secretly surrounded by people from ancient legends? Gods and spirits who really exist and still live and walk around on this planet? Even though they lived thousands of years ago?"

"That's about the size of it, yes."

"Let's not talk about size right now. I'm going to hardly

be able to walk for the next couple of days. Which brings me to my next question. Who are you, I mean, *really*?"

"I am Adonis."

Angie's eyes grew wide. "Adonis? You're telling me I've just been bedded by...by...by..."

"Yes, Angie Holland, of the twenty-first century. And for the record, you have no competition to worry about. No lover has ever surpassed your passion, your tenderness, your giving. I wish our lovemaking was not going to be limited to one encounter. but it must be this way."

Angie tried to stand. "Holy...and I can never tell. Even if I did, people would think I was completely, over the hill, crazy, out of my mind, meshuga bonkers!" Tears of joy rolled down her cheeks.

"Why would you want to tell?"

"Why? You're kidding, right? We call it bragging! Okay? Jesus, how I would love to tell my girlfriends that I got nailed by...*Adonis*! But..." Angie tried to wipe away the tears, but they kept coming. "So, where do we go from here?"

"Assemble your team. My job will come to an end soon. When it does, everything needs to be in place, ready to spring the trap."

"Okay, so, just for clarification; what '*precisely*' is your job?"

Dimitri rose and crossed to where Angie stood to gently dab at her tears with her towel. "My job is deceit. You see these tears? They are quite natural to you. They are not natural to our siren. She has never cried tears in her entire two-thousand-year existence. If she does, it makes her vulnerable. My job is to make her fall in love for the first time in her life and then break her heart. It isn't a very desirable job, but it is part of the formula to make her shield drop and put her in an emotional state so that she can be killed. Like it or not, it must be done."

Angie sat back down on the bed. "This is getting complicated. But okay, who else needs to be on the team?"

"You need a sacrificial victim. Someone who is willing to give their life so that others might live. And then, you need the executioner. This must be a male child below the age of puberty, because in her final moments, the siren may call upon her song, which would mesmerize an adult male and foil everything we have done up to that point. We will only get one chance. If we botch it, she may live for another thousand years. There is no telling how much destruction she will heap upon the earth, how many human lives she will take in that time."

Angie looked at Dimitri. The importance of her mission was taking on a new intensity. "I possibly have access to a male child. But where am I going to find somebody willing to put their life on the line? That's gonna be a tough one."

"Nobody said it was going to be easy."

"Save me the pithy remarks," Angie said.

———

A half hour later, Angie was dressed and ready to go. She and Dimitri left together and walked to the deck fronting the restaurant. Michael happened to be coming into the restaurant at the same time and saw them. Stretching out his hands, he rushed toward them as Angie sat at a table.

"You're here!" Michael said. "Why are you not in bed?"

Angie gave a nod toward Dimitri, who was getting seated. "This man's massage techniques are amazing."

"They must be," Michael said. "I never expected to see you walking around this soon. That's more than amazing. It's a miracle."

"More than you know," Angie mumbled under her breath.

"Well," Michael said, clapping his hands. "This calls for a celebration. We just got some fresh conchs in, and the guys in the kitchen have made some incredible 'Ceviche-a-la-Robert's Grove'. How about some, on the house, and cold beer to go with it?"

"Sounds like a plan," Angie said with a smile. She was feeling decidedly better, albeit with one part of her anatomy being a bit sore.

Ol' Jenkins was sitting at a table at the far end of the deck. He was quietly drinking his drink and looking out at the water, minding his own business.

When Michael walked away to alert the waiter, Angie began to quietly voice her concerns to Dimitri. "This whole magilla sounds like some kind of a Greek tragedy. It's an almost impossible set of circumstances. Who came up with this brain fart about needing a sacrificial victim? Are we absolutely sure that's necessary?"

"It's not a brain fart," Dimitri said defensively. "It is a part of—how would you modern humans say—the formula. For instance, a chemical formula isn't something that's up for discussion or debate. It just is. Combine one part hydrogen with two parts oxygen, and you get water. You can debate the subject until you're blue in the face, but at day's end, H2o translates to 'water'.

"Minerva was sent here to make sure you received the necessary information. I was sent here to cripple the siren emotionally. You are here to coordinate all of these parts in the 'formula' to accomplish what must be done. Any variance from the formula, no matter how slight, and it will be ineffective. Do you want to risk that?"

"Of course not," Angie snapped. "But where the hell am I supposed to find someone who is willing to end their life for the cause? Am I supposed to walk into a bar and announce, 'Hey! Any of you bar-fly mother fuckers want to cash it in for a good cause? All you have to do is be willing to have half of your head bitten off by a deranged, ancient creature; but hey, it'll be quick! Better than croaking slow of liver cirrhosis! Oh! And your death will mean something!

"That final act is going to be a humdinger, and I'm just having a hard time trying to come up with a list of possible volunteers. This is no easy task you two 'Ancient Greeks' have assigned to me."

Dimitri looked deep into her eyes. "If you were not who you are, if you were not what you are, have the intelligence that you have, or the courage that you have, we would never have chosen you. We have seen your mind at work. We have seen your determination, your heart. You, among the multitude, are one of the few on this earth who can do this. You are far more special than even you know. You walk among others, but yet, there is a glow around you. Now, go forward and believe in yourself as much as we do."

Angie looked at Dimitri and squinted. "'We' have seen? When the hell have you been watching me, and how?"

At that moment, Ol' Jenkins backed his wheelchair away from his table, turned and began pushing the wheels toward Angie and Dimitri's table. Angie spotted him moments before he bumped his wheelchair against her table.

"I'll do it," Ol' Jenkins said with finality.

"Beg your pardon? You'll do what?"

"You need someone to give their life up to that bitch-from-hell siren, right? I'll do it!"

Angie looked at Ol' Jenkins in disbelief. "You're willing to let yourself be killed by the siren? You do realize, being killed means there ain't no more. It's the last act of the play. Death is permanent. You don't get up and dust yourself off when the director says, cut!"

"Do you think I'm stupid, young lady?"

"So…you're willing to die?"

"Why not? My life ain't worth a shit, anyway. That bitch siren has already killed my daughter, and she's all I had to live for."

"I thought sharks got your daughter."

"Don't be naïve. Who do you think directed the actions of the sharks? Besides, I'm in this wheelchair because of her. She tried her best to kill me. Instead, she took away my life. What am I supposed to do the rest of my days, sitting in this infernal contraption? I can't walk, I can't make love to a woman. What woman would want me, anyway? I don't have anything left to offer. When I was a young man, I used to love waltzing with my wife, Helen. We were good dancers, too. We were good together, no matter what we did. Our daughter was proof of that.

"Then I got this weed up my ass to come down here and get rich on black coral. It seemed so 'adventurous' at the time. Black coral is in high demand, still gets a good price, even today. The cost for that was, I lost everything. Everything! Now, I don't even have Helen to go home to. If I was in a city, I'd be that old derelict you see sitting on a park bench, feeding the pigeons. Can't do that around here. We don't have pigeons; just these infernal, God-forsaken seagulls. Can't feed them. They thank you by crapping on your head. Flying rat bastards!"

"So, you need someone to feed to the siren, you've got someone. I'm ready to get this shit over with. I'm hoping there is a hereafter so that I can join my daughter. That one thing would make it all worthwhile. Everybody has to die sometime. This is my one chance to make my death count for something. Eh? Ol' Jenkins gonna give 'em a big finish. Surprise, surprise! It'll make this miserable existence justified. No more living in a shoebox-sized room that smells like sweat. No more loneliness…"

Angie stared at him, trying to formulate the words to say to him. "You were all the way over there. There's a breeze blowing. How did you hear us talking?"

"I told you. Hearing is all I have left. I hear things that most people don't hear."

"Like what?"

"Well, I heard you two screwing like a couple of howler monkeys when I passed your room earlier. I've heard every conversation you've had about how to dispatch the bitch siren. That isn't important. Right now, you need to teach me what to do. From what I understand, there's some kind of a prayer, or a beseechment, a ritual that I have to recite before she puts the whammy on me?"

"Yes. You speak of dying so casually."

"Hmmm. I'm looking forward to it. Ain't so hard to die. It's living that's hard. Haven't you been listening? I'm tired of living this miserable, fucked-up life. I'm hoping Heaven will be better. If'n it ain't, I don't have much to lose. If you want to know the truth, I've thought about this fer a long time. Never wanted to commit suicide, because that goes against the Good Book. But this…I can perform a noble act as my very last goodbye. I think the man upstairs might bless me fer it."

Angie hadn't moved a muscle during the old man's speech. "Wow, Jenkins. I have a new respect for you. I never realized you have so much courage. Saying, thank you, hardly seems adequate. If this happens the way it's supposed to, you'll help save untold lives. Maybe thousands."

"Well, I outa get some brownie points fer that one."

Angie smiled. "I would certainly think so. Okay, here's what you'll have to do..."

For the next hour, Angie and Dimitri carefully went over every detail with Ol' Jenkins. Angie was surprised that the old man was a lot sharper than she had given him credit for.

"So, all this comes down from Greek Gods?" Jenkins asked when they had finished.

"Yes," Dimitri answered. "The formula is very ancient. We never thought it would have to be used. But now that we do, we must have mortals help us."

"Of course."

"Of course?" Dimitri said, looking at Jenkins. "Why, 'of course'?"

"Well, you're dealing with Texans here. That's slightly better than being a Greek God...with all due respect," he said with a teasing smile.

Dimitri laughed. "I believe I really am looking at a courageous man. You are facing certain death, and yet you make humor." He laughed again.

"Well, there you go," Ol' Jenkins said with a big smile.

Angie couldn't help but notice that the old man actually seemed relieved to know he would be dead within the next few days. She supposed that life really had been cruel to him. Death would put an end to his physical, mental, and emotional suffering. It really was a lesson to her to never take another person's heart for granted. Ol' Jenkins was a much deeper person than she had previously thought. He was probably a lot more intelligent than she had thought, too. She had underestimated the depth of his anguish, and now she felt bad about it.

On the other hand, he had solved a huge problem for her, and for the mission. She had been at a loss about what to do. Angie had never believed in the intervention of providence. Now she was beginning to have second thoughts. What had seemed insurmountable had evaporated before her eyes!

Wouldn't it be nice, she thought, if she could do something very nice for Ol' Jenkins? Sort of a thank you, as well as a going-away gift.

Suddenly, a helicopter could be heard incoming from the sea. At the same time, several cars began arriving in the Robert's Grove parking lot. People started bailing out of cars and walking toward the deck where Angie, Dimitri, and Ol' Jenkins were seated at a table.

James and Al Harmon emerged from some place. Angie looked up to see a man setting up a microphone over by the front of the restaurant.

"What the hell is going on?" Angie asked as James and Al joined the three of them.

Outside, the chopper landed and a tired-looking man in a white business shirt and blue trousers got out and started toward the restaurant. Reporters began to gather around the microphone. Angie wondered where they had they all come from.

A couple other official-looking men joined the man in the white shirt, standing beside him at the microphone. As the reporters waited, the man in the white shirt began to speak.

"I'm G.R. Bixler, head of the investigative team trying to figure out just exactly what happened at the Great Blue Hole that resulted in the death of seven Americans. This is basically an update, and the truth is, we don't know exactly what happened out there. We do know the victims were attacked by something. The question is, what was that 'something'? Because of the consistency of the wounds, we feel like whatever it was, it was a creature of higher intelligence.

"The problem is, it is also a dangerous creature that will most likely kill again, given the opportunity. For that reason, the government of Belize is shutting down the entire Lighthouse Reef area. No civilian traffic whatsoever will be allowed in. They are establishing barriers, even as I speak, at all access points, and notices are going out over all available media. No access, period. No exceptions. Lighthouse Reef and the Great Blue Hole are off limits until we kill or capture whatever did this."

"How do you plan on catching...or killing it?" a reporter asked.

"Good question," Bixler answered. "People are at work in a planning room at this moment, working on that problem. Even if I knew the answer to your question, I could probably not divulge it here, at this time. In any case, I am not directly involved in that aspect of it, so I do not have access to that information; at least for now."

Another reporter spoke up. "Why don't they just drop poison down in there? Not much else is in the hole, anyway. Might kill a few fish, but also, you might get whatever it is in the process."

Bixler looked disgusted at the suggestion. "I'm not even going to respond to that," he said. "No, wait. I will make a comment because the very idea makes me mad. Poisoning the Great Blue Hole would be one of the most reckless, most irresponsible, most catastrophic things people of intelligence and ethics could do. The likely fallout would affect miles of underwater caverns and kill untold wildlife. There is no limit to the amount of ecological damage that would be done. Poison the hole! I…are there any more questions? *Intelligent* questions?"

"What do you think your chances are of catching this thing?" a reporter yelled out.

The investigator shook his head. "I honestly don't know. We don't even know what we're looking for. Whatever it is, all we can do is hope it doesn't multiply and take up residency in some other location. I hate to think about something like that happening. In the meantime, we have seven families…well, actually, make that six families because two of the victims were from the same family, who want closure and justice. So far, we have been able to offer those families neither."

The press conference lasted a few more minutes, but nothing of significance was offered, and the news people dispersed feeling like they were going to have a hard time putting a meaningful report together from what little they had been given. One was heard to comment as he walked away, "I think they're holding something back. Maybe they're using us to throw whatever it is off track."

His colleague answered, "Throw what off track? If that's the case, we're talking about a human. That's the only thing that could be thrown 'off track'."

The two reporters looked at each other. The first one

said, "No—whatever it is, it is not a human. The killings are too diabolical. Not even a goddamned mass murderer does that to people."

As the two men walked away, Angie thought about their words. They were right. Not even a mass murderer would do that. And that reinforced her resolve to see this through, no matter what it took. The siren must be killed! And it was Angie's job to put all of the parts together, to make sure that happened, as planned, before she killed again. *Om Mani Padme Hum*! So be it.

CHAPTER TEN

Phone Call from Scott

The ceviche and beer had just arrived at the table when Angie's cell phone sounded. She retrieved it from the holder attached to her belt and pressed the answer button.

"Hello?"

"Hey, Baby! How are things going in Belize?" Scott asked.

"They're progressing," Angie answered. "How is Africa?"

"Well, what I've seen mostly is water. But now we've come ashore in Lamberts Bay, Western Cape, not the one in South Africa. Can you hear me all right?"

"I can hear you fine, although you sound very distant."

"Yeah, so do you! Hey, guess where my hotel room is?"

"Where?"

"It's in a cave! An actual cave. It's very modern, has a wide screen TV, WiFi, internet, big comfy bed, which I wish you were in. But it's inside a cave. They claim people used to hide in these caves back during the slave trading days. Bet they didn't have AC and wide screen then. Or international calling!"

"No, probably not. How's the shoot going?"

"Going pretty good. We've visited a lot of offshore islands. You wouldn't believe the sea birds—millions of 'em. I took at least a hundred pictures of gannets on this one island. Nature is amazing. Getting some unbelievable pictures, but none of them belong to me. They take my memory card at the end of each day and issue me a new one."

"Well, you're working for them. They want what they're paying for."

"Yeah, I know. I just wish a had a few of them for my collection."

"I'm sure you'll figure a way."

"Yeah…so, what's going on? You sound distant. And I don't mean just because of the phone."

"Sorry. It's probably the medicine. I had an accident. An old board broke on a pier and I fell through—hurt my back."

"Oh, my God! How bad is it? Are you in the hospital?"

"No. I was lucky. Nothing broken, but the doctor has me doped up a bit."

"Now, you have me worried," Scott said. "Look, we'll be through here in the next few days, and I'll come to you as fast as the airlines can carry me. I miss you."

"Miss you, too," Angie said. It was partly true. But she was so distracted by everything going on around her that she really didn't have time to miss Scott. And then, there was that interlude with Dimitri that had completely taken her breath away and left her drained like a sink! She feared that plain old sex would never be the same again.

"You sure you're all right?" she heard Scott's voice say.

"I'm sure. Quit asking that," she said, slightly irritated.

"Okay. Well, guess I'll go. I love you."

"I love you too, Scott. Be careful. Don't let those gannets bite."

"Yeah, okay. Bye."

"Bye!"

Angie hung up the phone, feeling guilty. She shouldn't have been so cold with Scott. After all, Dimitri had made it brutally clear that their tryst was a one-time event, *only*. Two ships that collided in the night. Scott would be by her side the rest of his life unless she messed up. Better to keep those home fires burning. Oh, shit! Here came the guilt. She could sense it knocking at the door to her soul.

She returned to the present and scooped a bit of ceviche onto a tortilla chip. When she bit down, she found the flavor was everything that Michael had promised.

From somewhere, Dimitri's voice came to her. "Pretty delish, eh?" He was sitting right next to her, but she had been so absorbed in her thoughts that she had closed herself off from everything and everyone around her. Now she was reemerging and realized that not only was Dimitri sitting at the table, but so were Al and James Harmon, and Michael had re-joined them.

Jesus! What's happening to me? she wondered.

"How's Scott?" James asked.

"What? Oh, he's fine. He's on the west coast of Africa. Some place called Lamberts Cove, or something like that. His hotel room is inside a cave. Anyway, he'll be back in a few days."

"That's good," Dimitri said. He was talking to Angie, but looking at the girl fifty yards away, standing on the pier, peering at him. It was Mara. When Angie looked at Dimitri, and then followed his gaze, she saw her, too.

"Your honey is waiting," Angie said with a hint of sarcasm.

"Yes. It appears she is frightened of coming here to the table to fetch me."

"Now, why would that be?" Al asked.

"Probably because she's afraid you would smell her," Dimitri answered.

"Smell her? What's that supposed to mean?" Michael asked.

"Mara is Maris in disguise. We all know that, right?"

There was a collective, "Yes."

"Basically, she is an animal. Animals go by smell. Therefore, they assume that humans do, too. Maris can change her appearance, but not her smell. She's afraid that if she gets too close, you will pick up her scent and know her true identity. So, she's keeping her distance to make sure that doesn't happen."

"Interesting," Angie said.

"I'd better go to her," Dimitri said as he got up from his chair. "Wouldn't want to fuck things up at this point!"

Angie had a dour look on her face as she watched him walk away.

———

True to her word, Angie did indeed get three sheets to the wind; to the extent that she had no recollection of returning to her room, or what time she did that, or under what circumstances. But when she woke up, sprawled across the bed, she found that her clothes were still on, so at least the odds that she had done something shameful…at least *sexually* shameful, were next to nonexistent. One debauch was quite enough. As good as it had been, Angie was struggling with guilt by now.

She dove into the shower, clothes and all. As the warm water ran over her from the shower head, she peeled off her clothes and threw them in the corner. She needed to feel clean, although she wasn't sure the shower would do it; but it would help. For now, she needed everything washed, inside and out.

An hour later, as she was getting dressed, she heard a commotion outside. Whatever it was, the timing was good because she was ready to leave her room and rejoin the outside world. Just as she stepped out the door, two reporter-types walked past her, talking to one another. "Harold said it's hideous. Nobody has ever seen anything like it!"

She could hear other voices coming from somewhere distant. As it turned out, there was a gathering on the dock. Somebody had hung some kind of creature up on a hook in a place that was normally reserved for taking trophy photos of deep-sea fish.

"Look at that bastard!" one man yelled.

"That sumbitch is uglier than my first wife," another man added.

As Angie got closer, she had to push her way through the throng to see what everyone was oohing and ahhing about. Once she got a clear view, she was at first stunned, then repulsed, both by the creature's appearance, and then by the horrific wounds the animal had endured at the hands of its captors. Dripping blood formed a pool beneath the animal, and part of its entrails hung on the outside of its body. It had large tentacles, equipped with huge suction cups, and round eyes as big as dinner plates with elliptical pupils, now stilled in death. The skin was mottled and gray. There was a stench emitted by the creature that was probably part of it before death.

"That's ghastly," someone said.

Just then, G.R. Bixler appeared and took up a position in front of the animal, while reporters and photographers took photos and bombarded him with questions.

"Is this the killer?" they all wanted to know.

"We aren't sure," he said answered loudly. "It is a killer. It is aggressive. It probably is the killer, but we won't know for sure before we perform some tests."

"What kind of tests, G.R.?" someone yelled.

"For one thing, we need to see if the teeth on this animal are the same kind of teeth that could have made the wounds on the victims."

"What kind of creature is that thing? Do you know the name of it?"

"No. We've never seen anything like it before. It's obviously a deep-water dweller. It could have been living in those underwater caves for eons."

"What about DNA?" someone else wanted to know.

"There's very little chance that any DNA evidence can be matched up. The victims were underwater for quite some time. Look, let me get out of the way so you can get your pictures. But let me make it very clear, we are not saying this creature killed those people that were aboard the yacht at the Great Blue Hole."

"Did you find it in the Great Blue Hole?"

"Yes, we did. It emerged from the grottos and tried to attack two of our divers. They defended themselves by shooting it with explosive-tipped spears in high powered spear guns."

Angie didn't need to hear anymore and turned and walked away. Her head hurt and she needed some breakfast. Poor assholes, she thought. When people are desperate, they will clutch at any straw. How strange that she knew the truth and she couldn't tell any of them. And now there were several reasons. One, they would think she was crazy. Two, it would blow the plan to kill the real killer out of the water. Life was a…conundrum, sometimes.

After a breakfast of ham and eggs, she decided to walk back down the beach to look at the old pier where she had her accident. A little more than twenty minutes later, she stood on the beach, looking at it. She saw where she fell through. A broken plank was still dangling precariously, swinging slightly in the breeze as if it would break away and fall at any second. It was like returning to the scene of a crime. This had been the starting point of what had led to her infidelity. Or had it? The truth was, she had wanted Dimitri before the accident ever happened.

Oh, God. There it was. The heavy feeling of guilt she had been trying to ignore; to sidestep. She knew the pain of violating a trust. It had happened to her, years earlier, in a different life. The dirty bastard she had given her heart to repeatedly made a fool out of her. There had almost been nothing left of her by the time it was over. She had fled the relationship, gasping and staggering, trying to find her identity again.

The experience had changed her, turned her into the person she was today—a little aloof to most people, until she got to know them; a cold, calculating business-woman who based all business decisions entirely on the potential for

ROI. She was successful to be sure, but there was something missing. Satisfaction? Fulfillment? A feeling of triumph, or even some kind of accomplishment?

The fact was, she was not who she wanted to be. And the tragedy was that she didn't know how to get there from where she was. These were emotions that she had shoved way down inside her, with a promise to deal with them 'someday.' Only that day always seemed to be tomorrow. Now, suddenly and without warning, tomorrow was here, and she wasn't prepared. She had violated her relationship with Scott, and she couldn't justify her infidelity, much less reconcile it in her mind and heart. Had she become that which she loathed from the center of her being?

She vowed to never repeat her mistake, and moreover, to keep it a secret, to not let Scott find out—ever. Just as she reached that point in her thoughts, the broken plank came loose and fell into the water with a splash beneath the pier, almost as a punctuation to her oath. She turned away and began walking back toward the lodge.

Arriving at the resort a little later, she noticed several new cars in the parking lot. Most of them had placards on the dash boards, or magnetic signs slapped on the front door panels identifying them as rentals, leased to TV or radio stations.

Some said 'K-something, something.' Others said, 'W-something-something.' It was a second-hand reminder of her failed love affair from years ago because the person she had given herself, and her virginity to, had been a radio executive. He had made the offhand comment one day that all radio and TV stations from east of the Mississippi had call letters that began with 'W.' Whereas, all stations from west of the Mississippi had call letters that began with the letter 'K.'

An almost interesting bit of trivia; but now she saw signs with both letters on the various vehicles. Great—this story was going to gain international attention if they kept it up. That wasn't going to make things any easier, with a cluster of reporters around. The siren might panic and decide to go underground. Well, under 'water.' After visually scanning the cluster of vehicles, Angie turned and headed for the bar.

When she arrived, she found that almost all of the outside tables were taken. Ol' Jenkins was over to one side, watching the array of men and woman, cackling to himself. Even so, he seemed like the lesser of evils, so Angie joined him.

When she sat down next to him, he leaned forward so he could speak low enough not to be heard. "Heh, heh, this is the shits, ain't it? All these mother fuckers down here because they seen that picture of the sea creature. Half of 'em are pissed off because they didn't get to scoop the story."

"How do you know that?"

"I been listening to 'em. They're a competitive bunch of pricks."

Angie looked around at the several women also in attendance. "Looks like not *all* of them are pricks."

"I've been listening to them talk. Trust me, they're pricks! That broad over there in the blue blouse taught me some words I didn't know. And I think she's an on-camera reporter."

"Really?"

"An' that guy sitting there in the red blazer... it oughta

be pink, because he's so queer he could change a nine-dollar bill into three threes."

"Jenkins!" Angie scolded.

"Yeah, I know, I know. This is just a news report. I ain't editorializing."

"Trust me, you were editorializing!"

"Well, maybe a little. Anyway, they're also pissed off because they came down here to see that creature and get pictures of it, and it's not here anymore. Good thing, too. It'd be stinking like a New Orleans whorehouse at low tide by now."

"Where is it?"

"Dunno. They took it down, put it on the back of a boat. Probably took it some place where they could perform tests on it to see if it's really the killer."

"Yeah, good luck with that," Angie said. She studied him for a few moments. "Jenkins, do you ever leave this deck?"

"Yeah, when I'm too exhausted to think. Don't like to go home much. I live in a shoebox-sized room. Ain't nothin' there except a cot. I ain't got no TV anymore. I hate being there. All the shit that goes on here is my entertainment. And believe me, the crap that goes on here sometimes is better than any TV show."

"I believe that," Angie said.

"You put on a pretty good show yourself, last night," he said with a laugh.

Angie's eyes got wide. "Oh, dear God. What did I do?"

"Whoa!" Jenkins said. "I shouldn't a said nothing. Jest fergit it."

"Like hell," Angie protested. "You're the one who opened this can of worms. Now tell me the truth. What did I do?"

He hesitated for a moment. "Well, uh, you got on a rant 'bout men. Said all they wuz, wuz a bunch of dicks with legs. Then you grabbed one of the waiters by the crotch and squeezed real hard, which put him out of commission for the next hour. Dr. Maurine wuz pretty put out with you. Tried to calm you down. Then you asked a female reporter at the next table if she had ever tried to suck a dick that was too big to get in her mouth. Dr. Maurine wuz ready to shoot you at that point, but you said, 'Wait! I know where one is that's that big!' That's when Dr. Maurine got you up and steered you toward your room. That wuz pretty much the end of the show, but I'm surprised you didn't get a standing ovation from some of those reporters."

"Oh Jesus," Angie said, holding her face in her hands. "How many people were out here?"

"I dunno. Maybe a dozen."

Angie made a guttural sound into her hands. "Oh, dear God, dear God, dear God. That explains why, when I ordered breakfast this morning and told the waiter I wanted my eggs fried, he said, 'I thought you preferred them scrambled.'"

Ol' Jenkins laughed and tapped Angie on the shoulder. When she looked at him, he motioned toward a female reporter who had just joined some of her associates at a table. The reporter glared at Angie for a moment, then looked away.

"Is that her?" Angie asked, as if she needed confirmation after the look she had gotten.

"Yup."

"I've got to apologize," she said, getting up from her chair.

Angie walked over to where the woman was seated with two male reporters. Lowering her eyes, she said, "Ol'

Jenkins there, just told me what I did last night. I...it snuck up on me. I haven't been that snockered since my college days. I mean, that's no excuse. But I am sorry. You have no idea how sorry. I apologize."

The woman stared at her, her hands folded, but said nothing. Without further comment, Angie turned away and started back to her table, where Jenkins was waiting. She had only gone a step or two when the woman called after her, "You said that you knew where a dick was that was that big."

Angie turned and looked at the reporter. After a moment, the woman asked, "So, did you suck it?"

Angie felt like that remark made them even. She said nothing, just turned and continued walking back to her table.

———

Angie was worried. If Scott found out about this, her goose was cooked. The truth would tear his heart out. He was a very sensitive person, anyway. That's part of what made him such a good photographer. His reaction would be like the eruption of a volcano, and Angie would find herself walking down the road with her suitcase in hand. What in the hell had compelled her to...oh, what the hell. Too late to cry over spilled milk now. Instead, she needed to go into damage control mode.

She had really created a magilla for herself when her absolute total concentration needed to be on fencing in that bitch siren and cooking *her* goose! She was the evil one, right? All Angie did was give in to her pent-up passion. Crap. She had to forget about it; think about something else.

Coming back to the present, she saw Dimitri approaching. He sat down and looked around.

"Where did all these people come from?" he asked.

"Their excuse for being here is that they're reporters. The real reason they're here is because they're morbid curiosity seekers. Being reporters is just a thin justification, a disguise. They came to see the sea creature, which isn't here anymore; so their trip is a bust unless somebody comes up with another sea creature."

"Not likely," Dimitri said. "There are only a couple of monsters like that on the whole planet. Now, there is one less."

"That's sort of a strange thing to say," Angie said, squinting at him.

"Haven't you figured out the identity of the sea monster?" he asked, looking at Angie, then at Jenkins.

"Identity? What do you mean, 'identity'?"

"I mean exactly that. 'Identity.' That sea creature they killed was Maris's father."

"What?"

"Yeah. He must have known his daughter was up against it, so he came here to help her. Problem was, he was just as naïve as his daughter. And apparently didn't have the resilience she has. Mara has been pining all day. When I inquired, she said she had 'received word that a close relative had died.' But it's plain that she is hurting deep inside. This plays perfectly into our hands."

"How do you mean?" Angie asked.

"She's had a hard emotional blow. Now, when I lower the boom on her, the chances of her springing a leak are all the better." Dimitri smiled.

"How is that part of the plan going?"

"Couldn't be better," Dimitri said. "She's in love with my Johnson. The siren found her match and can't get enough."

Angie wanted desperately to make a comment, but restrained herself.

"Now all I have to do is begin to convert some of that lust into honest emotion—*love*."

"How are you going to do that?"

"I'm not sure. So far, I have managed to create human emotions in her, such as missing me when I'm not with her. So, love can't be that far away. It all has to do with keeping her away from the water. She appears befuddled even when she's no more than a hundred feet from the marina, for instance."

Angie looked across the deck at nothing in particular. "Geez, are all men this calculating?"

"Most," Dimitri said. "Men are natural hunters. Being calculating is a part of tracking. So yeah, it would be almost against their instinct to not be."

Angie looked at Dimitri. "Good to know," she said.

CHAPTER ELEVEN

A Gift for Ol' Jenkins

Something had been bugging Angie ever since the moment that Ol' Jenkins had volunteered his life in the cause to save other lives. He deserved a thank you. Not just a thank you, but a meaningful thank you—a memory to take with him when he left this world.

So, in typical Angie Holland style, she set out to arrange just such a memory. She sought out Dr. Maurine Howard for a consultation.

"Are there any women around Placencia that have good hearts, but maybe, loose morals?"

"What do you mean?" Maurine asked. "Hookers?"

"Well, yeah, hookers. But I'm after a very special kind of a hooker."

"A lesbian hooker?"

"What? No! Oh, Jesus wept, no! It's not for me. It's for Ol' Jenkins."

"You want to get Ol' Jenkins laid? I don't think he can."

"Not necessarily laid," Angie said. "But I do want him to have what might be described as 'an interlude' with a woman. It needs to be somebody who will be tender, patient and understanding. Someone who will lie naked with him in bed and…well, you know. But also, talk to him. That old man is so lonely. I just want to do this one nice thing for him."

"Okay," Maurine said. "I won't even try to guess at your motives. But I think I know one woman who might fill the bill. Her name is Marijane. You want me to try to call her?"

"No. I want to set this up as a surprise. If she agrees to it, I want to rent one of your rooms for Ol' Jenkins and pay for it for the next couple of weeks. He told me he lives in a shoe- box-sized room that smells like dirty socks. He deserves better."

"Uh, huh. Okay, let me get my keys. We'll take my car."

———

Forty-five minutes later, Maurine and Angie sat in a café, at a small metal table, talking to a fading beauty in her late thirties named Marijane Caulker. Angie's instructions were explicit; and her pay would be generous—one thousand American dollars. Marijane was agreeable and delighted.

"You say dis mahn can't even get it up?" Marijane asked.

"I'm not sure, but probably not," Angie answered.

"Dein, how am I supposed to please him?"

"By being kind to him. Talk to him. Lay naked with him in bed and rub your hands on him. Do what you would do if you were in love with him."

Marijane smiled. "I tink I got de picture. I gonna make Mr. Ol' Jenkins very happy!"

Their deal being sealed, Marijane grabbed a couple of things and got in the car with Dr. Howard and Angie.

Minutes later, she was escorted into a room at Robert's Grove and asked to wait for a few minutes. While she waited, she made herself at home, determined that she would try to make the old man smile a smile that would last him a lifetime.

Meanwhile, Dr. Maurine and Angie sought out Ol' Jenkins. Sure enough, he was sitting in his favorite spot, out on the deck, drinking a beer and looking out at the sea. When he heard the footsteps of the two ladies, he looked up at them and smiled. "Good morning, ladies. What brings you to Paradise?"

"The Paradise is yours today, Jenkins," Angie said, as she grabbed the handles on his wheelchair and turned him in the opposite direction from the table.

"Where you taking me?" he demanded.

"I have rented a room for you here at the resort," Angie said. "You're fixing to move out of that cobweb infested flea trap you're living in."

"What? Oh, my Lord! What has Providence seen fit to bestow upon me?" he exclaimed as Angie wheeled him toward his room along with Dr. Maurine.

Angie patted him on the shoulder. "I don't know how much Providence has to do with it, but don't worry, just enjoy."

"What about my stuff?"

"The stuff in your room? How much stuff do you have?"

"Well, not that much, actually. But there are a couple of things..."

"You have plenty of time to worry about that later. Besides, we have somebody who'll be happy to help you with your 'stuff'," Dr. Maurine advised.

When they arrived at his room, Dr. Maurine opened the

door and Angie wheeled him in to see Marijane, who was standing there with a big smile. "Good mahning, Mr. Jenkins. Welcome. Come in. Let me help you with your bath."

Ol' Jenkins was speechless. He looked at Angie and Dr. Maurine, as they headed to the door and closed it behind them.

In the hallway, Dr. Maurine confided to Angie, "I think that is a done deal." Heading out to the bar, she added, "You're a good soul."

CHAPTER TWELVE

The Obsidian Dagger

Dimitri stood with an apparently grieving Mara as they looked out to the sea. "I'm sorry for your loss," he said. "Were you close to this person?"

"I was…a long time ago," she responded.

"Umm." He put his hands on her shoulders. "Who was it, exactly?"

"It doesn't matter." She turned to face Dimitri. "As long as I have you, I can endure anything."

"What does that mean?" Dimitri asked. "Is that your way of saying that you love me?"

She looked deep into his eyes. "Well, I certainly love that huge thing of yours. As for the rest of you…yes, I think I do. It's a strange feeling. It's the first time I've ever been in love."

"Really?" "Wow, that's super." He embraced her as she hugged him back. Releasing her, he peered down at her face. "It's a beautiful day. Let's go for a swim."

Mara pulled away. "No, not right now. Maybe later. I

think that right now, we should go to your room and 'celebrate' me admitting my feelings to you."

Dimitri nodded. "Ohhh, yes. That's certainly something to celebrate."

She took his hand and led him toward his room at Robert's Grove.

———

Two hours later, Mara was sated and drowsy. Dimitri got up, stretched, and announced that he was going to the bar to get them drinks. When he left the room, he went instead straight to the pier behind the resort where Angie stood watching Al, who was fishing.

Dimitri hurried down the pier to join them. "It's time to get the kid down here,"

"What kid?" Angie asked.

"James's brother. This whole thing will collapse in front of our eyes without him."

"Oh, shit," Angie said, and grabbed her cell phone.

———

The next afternoon, Al, James, and Angie were waiting at the small municipal airport for the arrival of Mrs. Sally Harmon, and James's little brother, Stevie. When the plane's door opened, and James's girlfriend Athena appeared, James's face lit up with pleasure.

"Surprise!" she called out and waved, seeing him.

James rushed up the boarding stairs to take her hand and help her down the steps. "Wow!" he said. "What a wonderful surprise. Whose idea was this?"

"Mine," his mother replied from the step above. "You're fourteen. I figured we women need to get an early start on training you." Everyone on the tarmac laughed. James gave Athena a big hug, and they all headed to the limo to take them to Robert's Grove. The new arrivals were treated like royalty as they were ushered into the van. Sally Harmon appeared to be thoroughly confused by all the hubbub.

"What is so urgent?" she wanted to know. "And why is it so vitally important for Stevie to be here?"

"It's a *lonnng* story," Al Harmon said with a strained smile. "Welcome to Belize. Did you bring your bathing suit?"

"No. I didn't have time. You said we needed to get to the airport right away. I only had time to throw a few things in—"

Al waved off her apology. "It's all right. Not a problem. I know you like to shop. They have a great boutique at the resort, plus there's all sorts of stores all over Placencia. You're going to have a field day here, finding all kinds of nice things!"

Sally's eyes widened with interest. "Really?"

"Oh, yeah! There are shops here that specialize in European fashions. You're gonna love it here. Have a ball."

"Okay, but I still don't understand why we're here. And it seems so urgent. What on earth is so urgent?"

"I'll explain it all to you when we get to the resort," he promised. Then, under his breath, he said, "But first, I'm gonna have to get you three sheets to the wind so you don't freak out."

When the van pulled up in the parking lot of Robert's Grove, Al helped Sally with her luggage and led her to their room for her to freshen up, while James took Athena and Stevie, and headed for the restaurant.

"Come on, Stevie," James said. "Wait till you try the fish tacos they have here. Oh, and I need to tell you a story about our family history, because we have a special, super job for you to do." Putting his hand on Athena's shoulder, he said, "I'm super happy that you're here. But I need for you to brace yourself."

"What do you mean?" Athena asked.

"Well, you've walked into the middle of something here that I never really wanted you to know about. Now that you're here, there isn't much choice. So…"

"Are you talking about the siren?"

James's mouth dropped open. "Yeahhh. How did you know?"

"You told me all about it when you came back from Belize two years ago. Don't you remember? Then you made me promise to never bring it up, so, I never did."

"Wow. I don't remember that. But I'm glad I did, because that will give you a leg up on understanding some things you're going to hear today."

"She's come back, hasn't she?"

James blinked. "How did you know that?"

"I'm Greek," she said with a smile. "Besides, it's all over the TV. If you know the history of it, such as I do, it doesn't take much to connect the dots."

James smiled as he squeezed Athena's hand. "I've got sommme girlfriend!"

In the restaurant, Al sought out Dr. Howard to ask her to show Sally around while he and James had a long and meaningful talk with Stevie. Al was apprehensive at first about Athena being present, but James managed to iron out that wrinkle in no time.

"What do you want me to do?" Dr. Howard asked.

"Keep her occupied in the gift shop, the boutique; give her a couple of those Siren's Juice drinks, or whatever it's called, to loosen her up. Just keep her away from James, Stevie, and me for at least an hour. Longer would be better. Maybe go shopping with her at some other stores. Get her talking about cooking. That woman loves to cook." Al turned to Athena. "Would you like to go with Dr. Howard to help keep my wife distracted?"

"No," Athena said firmly. "I want to be here and learn what's going on."

Dr. Howard broke in to say, "Okay, so basically, spend the day shopping? I can do that." She turned toward Athena. "You sure you don't want to come shopping with us?"

Athena shook her head. "Thank you, but I'd like to be here with my boyfriend. The toot keeps running off to all the tropical places without me."

"Okay," Al said. "It's all set. Thank you, Maurine." He turned and walked off toward the restaurant with James, Stevie, and Athena.

When they arrived, James picked a table farthest away from the bar and the other tables where guests might sit when they entered, while Al went to the bar to order drinks and botanas. When he returned to their table, his two sons were deep in conversation, with Athena listening intently. He sat down to join them. "How far have you gotten?" he asked James.

"I told him about our ancestor, but he already knows about that."

"Okay, good." Al looked at Stevie. "What you don't know is that a couple of years ago, your brother had a life and death confrontation with the siren. He shot her in the chest with a bang stick."

Stevie's face lit up. "You really did that, James? You shot somebody with a bang stick?"

"Not just 'somebody,'" James corrected. "I shot *the siren*."

"Shot her twice," Al said. "Apparently, it didn't kill her. But she *must* be killed. Here's why…"

For the next hour, James and Al took turns filling in the younger Harmon on the Harmon family legend, the efforts to kill the siren, and why it was absolutely necessary that this effort be made. They had to impress upon Stevie that although the siren looked human, she was not. So, it would not be considered murder, or a bad thing, to kill her. They also explained what the alternative might be if their mission failed. Therefore, it could not fail.

Much more than the Harmon family honor depended on this twelve-year-old boy sinking a knife into the siren at precisely the right moment, in precisely the right place in her body, to kill her. They also explained the reason *they* couldn't do it, whereas, because of his age, *he* could.

By the time Al and James had brought Stevie up to speed, the boy felt he was ready. "You can depend on me," he announced. "I am a Harmon. It is my honor and duty to keep the respect of the family name." Al and James looked at one another and nodded. Stevie was ready.

"This time, she's going down," James said with

confidence to his father. Stevie smiled and nodded in wonder.

Athena leaned forward to speak confidentially to Al. "Excuse me. I realize I'm an 'outsider', but I have to tell you something. I happen to be a student of Greek mythology. When I go to college, that will be my major."

"Okay," Al said. "I'll accept your 'credentials'. Besides, we need all the help we can get. So, what is it? Do you think we're missing something here?"

"The knife," Athena said. "You just said, 'knife', and it can't be just any knife. That's why the one that Captain Hughes stuck in her back didn't work. It has to be a special knife."

Angie had just come into the restaurant, and seeing the group, came over to their table. "Oh, save me!" she said, exasperated. "Another special 'something' to stir into this stew? What's next? Eye of newt?"

"I'm sorry," Athena said apologetically, standing up as if getting ready to leave the table. "I didn't want to say anything, but the fact is, if you don't use the prescribed kind of dagger, the siren will survive the attack and all of your efforts will have been for nothing."

Angie sighed, shaking her head. "Okay, exactly what is the 'prescribed' kind of blade? And how do you know so much about this shit, anyway?"

Athena got a faraway look in her eyes. "The blade cannot be made of steel. The siren has spent the past two thousand years in the land of the Maya Indians. Therefore, it will take something 'Mayan' to stop her."

"Such as?"

Athena did not speak for several seconds, still looking out into space. "Obsidian. The entire dagger must be made of obsidian—even the handle. You must obtain what is known as an 'Athame'."

Angie rolled her eyes. "This is getting too crazy."

Athena shook her head as if to clear it, then took her seat again.

"Obsidian?" Al repeated. "I know quite a bit about obsidian. It's a very hard, volcanic glass. It was a top-shelf trade item with the ancient Maya. They made knives from it, even way back then. Matter of fact, they were usually sacrificial knives. The old Maya kings were big on cutting hearts out and holding them up to the sun. I seriously doubt that the sun gave a damn. Weird religion. But now that I think about it, I have a friend who collects Mayan artifacts, and I think he has one of those old knives. Athena, do you think that would work?"

"What? A knife of obsidian from antiquity?"

"Yeah," Al said. "A knife from antiquity. Or as you put it —a dagger."

"Yes," Athena said. "That would work as good as an athame."

"From the mouths of babes," Angie said, softly.

"I need to call Ben," Al said, reaching for his cell phone and pulling up his contacts. Ben was apparently a good friend, as his number was there. He clicked on the name for the number to be called. After a few moments, Al said, "Ben, it's me, Al. Yeah, how's it hanging?…Well, funny you should ask. I need a favor and I'm going to throw in a free trip to Belize if you say yes. You know that obsidian knife you have in your Mayan artifacts collection? I need it. Well, that's a long story. Come to Belize, we'll get disgracefully drunk and I'll tell you all about it. Are you kidding? They've got the best rum here in Belize to be found anywhere on the planet."

Al spoke with his amigo several more minutes. By the time the conversation was over, he was smiling, and Michael was on his phone, making plane reservations for Ben, and reserving a room for him.

Now the executioner was in place. The lover was in place and doing his job to bring her to her knees with futility. Amazingly, they had a sacrificial victim, ready and willing to lay down his life in this quest. What else?

The knife! It had seemed like something was missing, until thirteen-year-old Athena had arrived, and miraculously divulged vital information about the kind of weapon that must be used. That single factor could have rendered all other elements, including the death of Ol' Jenkins, as completely useless, without purpose. Now, all of the elements were accounted for and in their proper place.

Angie had done her job well. She had put all of those elements together; with a little bit of help from some ancient Greeks and one young, modern Greek. They were almost ready to spring the trap. It would be helpful if they could get a few of the nosy reporters to abandon ship. It wasn't going to help to have a crowd around when the crucial moment finally arrived. But now, the one other person they needed there was Al's friend, Ben, who would deliver the instrument of death.

Michael came back to the table. "When will he get here?" Angie asked.

"I pulled some strings," he said. "If he can get to the airport in Houston quickly enough, he can be here tonight."

"Tonight! Wow! Thank you, Michael. That's amazing."

"Well, I do what I can," he said with a smile.

"With a shiv for the siren," James said. "Thanks to my little Greek goddess, here." He winked at Athena.

"Amazing," Angie said. "A twelve-year-old is our executioner, and a thirteen-year-old pulled us out of the fire. Maybe our country isn't in as bad a shape as some people think."

———

While everyone was occupied going different directions, doing different things, James took Athena's hand and walked with her past the decking at the resort, and down to the beach fronting the marina. Coming to a palm tree that offered shade, he suggested they sit under it on the sand.

"It is so beautiful here," she commented after she sat down.

"Yeah, I know," he agreed, absently. "Athena, I can't tell you how glad I am that you're here. But I...first of all, how do you know all of that stuff? I mean, I've known you for several years now, and I had no idea."

"Don't get so excited, James. You know how you're always talking about the Harmon family this and that, legacy, legend, responsibility...well, I'm Greek. The Greeks and the Chinese are two of the oldest races on earth. We have our history. And my parents made sure that I received an education about my heritage, just like your family did. Except, there's more to my heritage. Our culture is responsible for the creation of things like mythology. I happen to find it fascinating. I'm proud to be Greek, so I really got into studying our race."

"You're like a walking dictionary, or something."

Athena laughed a little. "Looks like it came in handy today."

"Are you kidding?" James said. "Do you realize what you did in there? Your contribution means the difference between failure and success. What you did will result in thousands of lives being spared."

Athena lowered her eyes. "Right place, right time. I'm glad I was here to help, James."

"Well, I'm proud of you. My girlfriend. Wow!"

"Yep, I am. What is it, two years and counting?"

James reflected. "Yeah, and no end in sight. We, uh, make a good couple—boyfriend and girlfriend. I can't get over how you knew about that obsidian knife thing."

"I'm Greek, James. We have pathways to the past."

"Pathways?"

Athena stood up and brushed herself off. "It's not important. Come on, show me around a little. It's a beautiful day. I want to go see those stores over there."

James rose to his feet. "Ya know, when we get old enough, I'm going to fall in love with you. I mean, we're too young to talk about love now, but when we get a little older."

Athena took James by the hand and led him toward the stores a hundred yards distant. "James Harmon, sometimes you talk and make no sense at all. What makes you think we aren't old enough to feel emotions? Silly boy!"

James smiled and looked at Athena as they walked away. "Yeah? Wow! You aren't going to tell me, are you?"

"Tell you what?"

"How you knew about the obsidian dagger."

"Nope."

"That's what I thought. Well, it was worth a try."

"Yep."

CHAPTER THIRTEEN

Ben Young Comes to Town

They all had a meeting that evening in the restaurant that was designed to look like a casual get-together in case any eyes were watching that shouldn't be. Present were: the Harmon family along with Athena, Angie, Dimitri, and last, but not least, Ol' Jenkins.

Although Maurine Howard had successfully kept Sally occupied for as long as Al had requested, he still had sat his wife down in their room afterwards to give her a full explanation of what was being planned. Patiently and thoroughly, he answered her questions and tried to allay her fears. Although Sally had suspected something dire was afoot, she hadn't been prepared for anything that was as 'dire' as what her husband told her. The strange and awful nature of the whole truth did not sit well with a woman who was used to events like calm garden club meetings.

The waiter assigned to their table that evening was cordial, as always, but betrayed his caution whenever he got close to Angie. She had managed to apologize to him in private, beforehand, by explaining that when she had assaulted him, she had been under a lot of pressure, all of which he seemed to accept. But he was of the old school, believing in the maxim that once bitten, twice shy. The memory of having his gonads squeezed like lemons was still fresh in his mind.

Dinner went off without a hitch, with the conversation revolving exclusively around the final planning.

As they were finishing their meals, Angie placed her hands on the table and cleared her throat to get their attention. "It looks like everything is in place," she stated. Everyone nodded their approval, except Sally Harmon who was nervously fidgeting in her seat as she listened to Angie's pronouncements on how it would all go down. Although she had heard all the details of the plan from Al, she continued to nervously hold up a finger, ready to speak, to question the appropriateness of the act and how it could be carried out successfully. She couldn't grasp a scenario wherein someone's murder was plotted and everybody else seemed to agree on the plan and to be perfectly all right with the outcome. Sally repeatedly dabbed at her mouth with her napkin between bites of her Grouper a la Placencia, but it was doubtful that she tasted much of anything as she was too preoccupied with her thoughts.

Angie lifted her chin toward Dimitri. "What time do we need to be ready to go?"

"Right at 2:00 a.m.," he answered. "Mara likes her usual, nightly yum-yum, then she wants to go walk by the water. I think she needs to drink sea water to wet her gills."

Sally Harmon wrinkled her brow. "Gills?" she said.

Al leaned over to her. "Not here," he whispered. "I'll explain it to you in the room."

Dimitri continued. "This time I'll go with her when she

goes walking and propose marriage. She is bound to be cornered by that and make a confession. That's when I will act shocked and drop the bomb."

"Bomb?" Sally asked, blinking slowly in disbelief.

"Hush!" Al cautioned under his breath. "I'll explain the whole thing to you in a little while."

"Watch for my signal," Dimitri said to the others. "I'll be looking for her to cry. 'If' that happens, it's the ideal time to pull the trigger."

"Trigger?" Sally Harmon again repeated his word in disbelief.

Al held a finger to his lips while shaking his head. "Not now."

Dimitri went on, non-plussed. "Jenkins, that's when you will be on stage. I'm sorry about the outcome for you... but just know there is a hereafter and you will be free of that wheelchair for eternity."

With that, Sally snapped. "Hold on!" she said loudly, her voice quavering. "Are you talking now about someone else being killed?"

"Yeah...me," Jenkins answered, evenly, with a small smile on his lips.

Sally cried out, "Oh, horrors! Good God. This is just too much. This is, this is, *insane!*" With that, she pushed her chair back and stood, then threw her napkin on the table and left in a rush, exiting the restaurant.

"She didn't seem to handle that too well," Stevie Harmon said.

"So, anyway," Dimitri continued, ignoring Sally's outburst, "your death should be almost instantaneous; not much pain at all. And if there is pain, it will be over in the blink of an eye. We all want to thank you for your sacrifice,

Jenkins. What we are attempting to do would not be possible without you." He held out his hand toward Jenkins in recognition.

"Well then," Jenkins said. "Let's make this a party. A man should go out in a blaze of glory, and never completely sober."

"Hear, hear," Al said, raising his glass. The rest of the party raised theirs toward Jenkins.

It was at that precise moment that a new voice was heard at the entrance to the restaurant. "Just wait a damn minute," Ben Young boomed.

Everybody twisted their heads around to see who was speaking. "I just heard the magic word, 'party.' I've come down here all the way from Houston, and I'm thirsty. So, that party had better include me."

Al quickly rose from the table. "Ben Young. You old horse thief. Damn, it's good to see you. Get yourself in here. Uh, it just so happens we have a fresh opening right here next to me." Al indicated the seat that Sally had just abandoned. "Sit, sit!" Then he motioned to Harold, the waiter. "Harold, get this man a drink. He's come a long way—and make it strong. He's got some catching up to do."

"Right away," Harold responded and headed toward the bar without asking what it was that Ben Young wanted to drink. Once Ben called after him what he'd like, the party began in earnest. Ben and Al had to trade greetings and stories for a half hour before they settled down and started talking about the reason for bringing the obsidian dagger to Belize.

As Al carefully explained what was going on, Ben sat frozen-faced, holding onto his drink and not blinking. When

Al had reached a stopping place, Ben emptied his glass and held it up so Harold could see. "I need another drink."

Ben looked incredulously at Al for a long moment. When his new drink arrived, he took a long swallow, then said, "If it was anybody besides you, I'd have left the table at the point where you started talking about killing somebody. But...goddammit, I've known you for more than twenty years and I remember you saying something about this a couple of years ago when you had your arm in a cast. But I'll tell you what—if I live to be a hundred, I know I'll never hear another tale anywhere close to this one."

"Yeah, the problem is," Al said, "this is no tale. We're involved in something here that's very serious. Human lives depend on the outcome of what happens or doesn't happen here within the next twenty-four hours. We've got all these prescribed rules that we've got to follow, and apparently, one of the key elements is that we have to use an obsidian dagger to kill this thing."

"Well," Ben said, "I brought it. It's in my bag, in my room."

"Come on," Al said, slapping Ben on the shoulder. "I'll walk with you to go get it."

CHAPTER FOURTEEN

End of an Epoch

A t two a.m., when all the world was quiet, a sexually-sated Mara walked hand-in-hand with her handsome Greek boyfriend from his room to the dock fronting the marina. They made small talk as they walked and Mara giggled at something Dimitri said.

Any casual observer would have thought they were a typical couple enjoying a normal evening. But, deep in the shadows made by the full moon, several people watched intently and waited for what they hoped would happen in the next few minutes. Some were players in this drama of life and death. Others were observers with a vested interest; but they all watched and waited with equal apprehension, fingers crossed that everything would unfold according to plan.

The dew glistened in the moonlight, covering everything. Crickets and small tree frogs sang their symphony and aromas from the night flowers filled the air along with the salt air from the crystal blue Caribbean. The night was peaceful, pastoral, and tinged with the light magic that can only be felt at certain times past midnight.

As Dimitri and Mara neared the dock, he bent down close to Mara. "Did you mean it when you said that you love me?"

Continuing to gaze out at the water, she said, "Yes, I did. For the very first time in my life, I know what love feels like. It's strange and a little frightening, but also very sweet."

She released his hand, then hopped from the pier to the stern of a yacht that was moored there, climbed down the ladder to the dive platform, got on her knees and dipped her hand into the salt water and smeared it on her face. She laughed, and said by way of explanation, "I've always wanted to do that!" Giggling, she returned to Dimitri.

He put his arm around her slender waist and cooed, "Yes, well, I love you too. That being the case, I think we should take this relationship to the next level. What do you think?"

"What do you mean?" Mara asked innocently, turning from him and placing her hands on the railing of the dock.

Dimitri stood close behind her and whispered in her ear, "It's natural progression. What I mean is, I want more. If you really mean it when you say that you love me, then we should live together. Make a life together. I want to marry you. Mara. Will you marry me?"

Mara was stunned. She hadn't expected this, nor did she see it coming this evening. Her mouth dropped open as she turned to look into his eyes. "What?"

"Marry me," he repeated. "We should have a family—you know, a house with a white picket fence, walk-in closets, two dogs, and a barbeque pit in the back yard. A little later, a couple of little ones playing at our feet; at least one boy and a girl."

"What are you talking about?" Mara gasped. "I can't marry you."

Dimitri's face fell. "Why not? You say that you love me. I love you. It's simple. That's what people do. They make a life together."

Mara was quiet for several moments, thinking how to talk her way out of this, but no story came to mind. Finally, she said, "I can't. I just can't."

Dimitri pushed out his lower lip and turned away from her, wondering if he was convincing her of his disappointment.

Mara gently put her hand on his shoulder. "I'm sorry. It just cannot be."

Dimitri turned back to face her; his face distorted with emotion. "I want to know why. This is confusing. You say that you love me, and yet, I'm hitting a brick wall. Is there someone else?"

"No, no. That's not it at all."

"Then, what? What you're saying makes no sense."

Mara swallowed hard and looked down. "Okay. Because I love you, I'll show you. And showing you what I am about to show you will prove that I love you. Look at me…no, wait. Don't look at me until I tell you to."

Dimitri ignored her instruction and, reaching out, tilted up her chin to look her in the eye. The vision before him began to grow wavy, the colors blurred and became scrambled. When the image sharpened, it was Maris he was facing instead of Mara.

"Because this is who I *really* am," she said.

Dimitri took a step back as his eyes grew wide, staring at this other woman. "What just happened? Who the hell are you? *What* are you?"

"My name is Maris," she said.

"What happened to Mara?"

"I am Mara. I have been in disguise. What you see before you is who I really am. This is my true identity."

"Disguise? I don't understand. Why do you need a disguise?"

Maris sighed. "It's very complicated," she said and turned away.

"Complicated? That's the wrong word," Dimitri said angrily. "To me, it looks like deception. I don't understand why you would need to pretend to be another person."

"I told you. It's very complicated."

"This is outrageous. I don't know why you needed a disguise. That sounds very suspicious. You're very beautiful. But now it seems like you're also a liar."

"Not without a good reason."

"There is never a 'reason' good enough to lie. Especially to your lover. You have deceived me, toyed with my heart, and used me. What else are you not telling me?"

Maris was becoming increasingly distraught. Then a look of hopelessness came into her eyes. "Okay. I have nothing to lose — well, that's not true; I have everything to lose. But I'll tell you everything, anyway." She pointed at the water. "I live there."

Dimitri appeared to be confused and upset. "There? What do you mean? Where the fuck is "there"? You mean, on the water?"

"No. *In* the water. *Under* the water."

"No shit? You live *in* the water! You live "*in*" the water? What does that mean? You can't marry me because you're a mermaid or something?"

Maris nodded, but now was close to tears. "Yes, and that's the reason I can't marry you, can't have your children. It's not because I don't love you, because I *do* love you. I've never loved before and I don't know how to handle these emotions. They're strange to me. I would marry you if I could. I swear it."

"*In* the water," Dimitri was saying incredulously. "I've fallen in love with a frigging mermaid! So, that means you can't have kids? We can't live in a house? No dogs? No barbeque pit in the back yard? No life that is just...*normal*? That's what I've wanted all of my life. Now you're telling me I can't have that if I continue to love you? No! I will not accept that. I'm sorry, but we can't go on under those circumstances. This relationship is over, Mara, or Maris— whatever your name is. You should have been truthful with me from the beginning."

Maris started to cry. The moment Dimitri saw tears running down her cheeks, he raised his arm and gave the signal to those waiting in the shadows.

Seeing the signal, Ol' Jenkins glanced around at the others. "Looks like I'm on. Thank you, everybody, for giving me some of my dignity back. I'll miss you." Then he wheeled his chair furiously toward the dock as fast as he could go. The wheels made a thump, thump as they crossed the planks on the dock.

"There you are, you fucking bitch!" he screamed at her when he drew close. "I thought I'd never see you again after you killed my daughter, you murderer from hell." He wheeled his chair to within a few inches from her.

Maris looked shocked. Where had this miserable pest come from? It was the middle of the night. She was having a talk with her boyfriend, trying to figure a way to work things out. She didn't need this pest bothering her. "Go away from me," she hissed, glaring at the old man.

"Fuck you," Jenkins said. "I'm fixing to slap the dog shit out of you!"

Maris screamed a primal scream that deepened into an animal growl as she reached down and grabbed Jenkins by the front of his shirt and threw him through the railing into the water.

She saw that Dimitri was still standing there and might try to stop her. Throwing back her head, she opened her mouth and began singing the beautiful, hypnotic song of the siren.

Dimitri barely had the will to signal Stevie, who came out of the shadows, running toward them, just as Maris turned and jumped into the water, on top of O'Jenkins. The top part of her body began to morph and became a grotesque, snaggle-toothed creature.

She opened her mouth to bite off the old man's head when he pleaded, "Wait! Don't I even get to say a prayer before you do this? I know you're gonna kill me. I don't care. But please, let me say one prayer."

"Hurry up," she growled.

"I beseech you, Argus Navis, and all the stars in your constellation; dispatch this minion of the devil. Slay this evil creature and send her back to hell where she belongs!"

Realizing that she had been tricked, Maris roared and bit down on his head. He writhed in pain, momentarily. Then a grating sound was heard as bone cracked and splintered under the pressure of her jaws. A pool of blood spread in the water, and Ol' Jenkins was no more.

At that moment, Stevie jumped into the water armed with the obsidian dagger and plunged it into Maris's back. She screamed in shock and agony before the siren's song was quelled. As instructed, Stevie pulled the dagger out, then plunged it in again, then again, and yet again, when he at last left it protruding from her back.

Maris managed to shrug Stevie off of her and, gasping desperately, managed to turn and grab hold of the edge of the dive platform on the rear of a yacht, the dagger still in her back. It was apparent that her wounds were mortal this time.

She laboriously pulled herself out of the water, up onto the dive platform, then managed to climb the ladder onto the boat. But she was growing weaker by the second. Al Harmon, who had been watching from the dock with Ben, stepped onto the boat, negotiated his way past Maris, and climbed down the ladder to the dive platform to help pull his son out of the water.

"Good job, son," he said to Stevie, as he lifted him onto the platform.

Dimitri stepped off of the dock and onto the boat to stand in front of Maris.

"Help me," she pleaded, reaching for him.

Dimitri pushed her hand away. "There is no help for you here. We are all here to see you die, so that the killing will stop. Your evil reign has come to an end, Maris."

The siren could no longer speak. She gasped and her skin began to discolor, turn ash brown, and become wrinkled. The wrinkling progressed for the next couple of minutes. In the end, she screamed a blood-curdling scream, turned into carbon, then fell into a pile of ashes on the stern deck of the yacht. She was no more—just a small pile of ashes that lay where the siren had stood.

"I'll be a sumbitch," Ben said as he stared at the residue that had been the siren. "You were telling the God's honest truth, huh, Al?"

Nobody else had much to say. Everyone just climbed

back up on the dock and walked slowly away. The last person to remain was Angie. She looked at the ashes and said, "Bitch! That'll teach you to mess with my boyfriend." Then she turned and walked away.

———

The next day, Angie was packing her suitcase in her room at Robert's Grove Resort as Scott sat and watched her.

"So, I rushed back here all the way from freaking Africa," he was saying, "because I was worried about you. You sounded so distant on the phone. I thought something was wrong. What was that all about?"

"I don't have a clue what you're talking about," Angie said, although even now, she seemed distracted.

"I guess it's just this thing with the siren?" Scott queried. "So, you say that's all over with? She's gone bye-bye for good this time?"

"Yep. The siren is no more."

"That's kind of sad, in a way."

"What is?"

"Well, you're a hero. You've prevented perhaps hundreds, maybe even thousands of people, from being killed. And yet, no one will ever know about it. The invisible hero—my invisible hero."

"There are no heroes, Scott. Just people who have a job to do and do it."

"Well now, that's just not true. You'll always be a hero to me."

Angie managed a half smile. "If that's true, then how about carrying this suitcase out to the van for your 'hero'?"

"Anything for my Angie," he said, grabbing the suitcase and following his girlfriend out the door. "I'm ready to go back to San Leon. I want some more biscuits and gravy. They don't know from zip about biscuits and gravy in Africa. They're too busy eating gannets!"

Don't miss out on your next favorite book!
Join the Melange Books mailing list at
www.melange-books.com/mail.html

Don't miss out on your next favorite book!
Join the Melange Books mailing list at
www.melange-books.com/mail.html

———

THANK YOU FOR READING

———

Did you enjoy this book?

We invite you to leave a review at your favorite book site, such as Goodreads, Amazon, Barnes & Noble, etc.

DID YOU KNOW THAT LEAVING A REVIEW…

- Helps other readers find books they may enjoy.
- Gives you a chance to let your voice be heard.
- Gives authors recognition for their hard work.
- Doesn't have to be long. A sentence or two about why you liked the book will do.

GEORGE DISMUKES spent the first half of his life in pursuit of adventure. This ranged from bullfighting as a youth to milking poisonous snakes professionally at Ross Allen's Reptile Institute in Silver Springs, Florida. The early 60s found him pursuing wild animals across the Serengeti in the movie business and operating an animal export company in Iquitos, Peru. He spent many years exploring archaeological sites of the ancient Maya Indians in Central America and studying their lost civilization. He also lived in Honduras, where the story, TWO FACES OF THE JAGUAR, THE LOST CITY, and THE JAGUAR'S QUEST take place.

In 1980, he began a video production company in Houston, Texas and worked as a 'triple threat' (writer/director/producer) creating some of the Houston market's most creative television commercials. He won a CLEO award for his production of a series of television PSAs concerning prevention of child abuse, funded through a grant from the University of Houston.

Currently, he lives on the Texas Coast with his soul mate and closest friend, Nadine, where he writes and works in magazine advertising. His hobbies include growing exotic chili peppers and experimenting with salsa recipes. Above all, George is a devout animal lover and advocate, fighting against animal abuse. He has two dogs, named Pulga and Gizmo, respectively.

🐦 twitter.com/@dismukesgeorge

ALSO BY GEORGE DISMUKES

Two Faces of the Jaguar Series

Two Faces of the Jaguar

The Lost City, Two Faces of the Jaguar

The Jaguar's Quest

Siren Song Series

Siren Song

Siren Song II

Siren Hunter